THE BRIDES OF BELLA LUCIA

A family divided by secrets, reunited by marriage

When William Valentine returned from the war, as a testament to his love for his beautiful Italian wife, Lucia, he opened the first Bella Lucia restaurant in London. The future looked bright, and William had, he thought, the perfect family.

Now William is nearly ninety and not long for this world, but he has three top London restaurants. He also has two sons, John and Robert, and grown-up grandchildren on both sides of the Atlantic who are poised to take this small gastronomic success story into the twenty-first century.

But when William dies and the family fights to control the destiny of the Bella Lucia business, they discover a multitude of long-buried secrets, scandals and the threat of financial ruin—but also two great loves they hadn't even dreamt of: the love of a lifelong partner, and the love of a family reunited....

Read the first two books of this compelling new miniseries and meet twin sisters: Rebecca Valentine, in **Coming Home to the Cowboy** by Patricia Thayer (Silhouette Romance), and Rachel Valentine, in **Having the Frenchman's Baby** by Rebecca Winters (Harlequin Romance). Be sure to see how this series unfolds in Harlequin Romance, starting in September 2006!

Dear Reader,

This month seems to be all about change. Just as our heroines are about to have some fabulous makeovers, Silhouette Romance will be undergoing some changes over the next months that we believe will make this classic line even more relevant to your challenging lives. Of course, you'll still find some of your favorite SR authors and favorite themes, but look for some new names, more international settings and even more emotional reads.

Over the next few months the company is also focusing attention on the new direction and package for Harlequin Romance. We believe that the blend of authors and stories coming in that line will thrill readers and satisfy every emotion.

Just like our heroines, my responsibilities will be changing, as I will be working on Harlequin NEXT. Please know how much I have enjoyed sharing these heartwarming, aspirational reads with you.

With all best wishes,

Ann Leslie Tuttle
Associate Senior Editor

Please address questions and book requests to:
Silhouette Reader Service
U.S.: 3010 Walden Ave., P.O. Box 1325, Buffalo, NY 14269
Canadian: P.O. Box 609, Fort Erie, Ont. L2A 5X3

PATRICIA
THAYER

Coming Home
to the
Cowboy

SILHOUETTE *Romance*®

Published by Silhouette Books

America's Publisher of Contemporary Romance

Special thanks and acknowledgment are given to
Patricia Thayer for her contribution to
THE BRIDES OF BELLA LUCIA series.

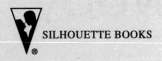 SILHOUETTE BOOKS

ISBN-13: 978-0-373-19826-9
ISBN-10:   0-373-19826-4

COMING HOME TO THE COWBOY

PATRICIA THAYER

has been writing for sixteen years and has published twenty books with Silhouette. Her books have been nominated for the National Readers' Choice Award, Virginia Romance Writers of America's Holt Medallion, Orange Rose Contest and a prestigious RITA® Award. In 1997, *Nothing Short of a Miracle* won the *Romantic Times BOOKClub* Reviewers' Choice Award for Best Special Edition.

Thanks to the understanding men in her life—her husband of thirty-plus years, Steve, and her three grown sons and two grandsons—Pat has been able to fulfill her dream of writing romance. Another dream is to own a cabin in Colorado, where she can spend her days writing and her evenings with her favorite hero, Steve. She loves to hear from readers. You can write to her at P.O. Box 6251, Anaheim, CA 92816-0251, or check her Web site at www.patriciathayer.com for upcoming books.

To the Valentine Ladies, Rebecca, Helen, Ally,
Linda, Teresa, Barbara and Liz...
Thanks for showing the new kid the ropes.
I've enjoyed working with you all, especially my twin,
Rebecca Winters, for giving me your time and expertise.
I value your friendship.

PROLOGUE

SHE had run out of time.

Rebecca Valentine stood at the large window overlooking Central Park. She'd worked hard to gain this big office and the junior partnership at the Pierce Advertising Agency. That had been her goal since college. It had taken ten years but she'd achieved it. In the meantime, she'd lost something she wanted even more.

She reread the official report from her recent medical tests. "The buildup of scar tissue caused by advanced stages of endometriosis… This condition highly decreases the ability to conceive. Surgery recommended."

In layman's terms, there would be no babies in her future.

Not that her OBGYN, Dr Shields, hadn't warned her for years to have a child early. And not that Rebecca had deliberately put it off. She just hadn't found a man to be a suitable father, and, of course, her career had contributed to the delay. But thirty-three shouldn't be too old to have a baby.

Deep down inside she'd wanted children. She wasn't sure she'd be good mother material, but now she'd never have a chance to find out. She'd never get the chance to feel a life move in her womb, nourish a baby at her breast, and give her child all the love she knew was so precious.

A tear escaped, and she wiped it away. Dr Shields had also informed her she was anemic and needed to slow down, get away from the stress of her job. The prescription had been for her to take some time off. How was she supposed to do that when she was responsible for no fewer than ten accounts? They were all important to her, especially now since all she had was her career.

There was a sharp knock on her office door and Brent Pierce poked his head in. The good-looking son of the agency's owner always had a smile for her. "Hey, Beck, have I got a proposition for you."

"Unless it involves relaxing on a beach somewhere for the next two weeks, I'm not interested. I'm overdue for a vacation."

"You, go on vacation?" He shook his head. "You'd be bored within two days."

"Brent, I've been working nonstop for the last six months. My doctor said I needed to take some time off. I'm anemic." That was all she was going to tell him.

He came into the room and sat on the edge of her desk. "So you'll eat a lot of red meat. I need you on this one, Rebecca. It's a new account for free-range beef." Suddenly his eyes brightened. "You know, I think there's a way we both can get what we want. You can still handle this new account and have your vacation, too." His smile widened. "How do you feel about exchanging a beach for a ranch in Wyoming?"

CHAPTER ONE

REBECCA looked out the window of the Cessna at the vast miles of majestic Rocky Mountain range. The brilliant May sun was reflecting off the dew-covered emerald-green pastures below.

Suddenly the plane dipped lower and she got a better look. The Tucker ranch came into view. Pristine white fences lined the road that led to a sprawling brick and white clapboard house trimmed with dark green shutters and surrounded by a perfectly manicured lawn. Her attention shifted to the outer buildings, several brightly painted red barns. In a large corral two beautiful white and black leopard-spotted horses, Appaloosas, ambled back and forth.

So this is Mitchell Tucker's Wyoming empire.

Rebecca felt the familiar stirring of excitement at the prospect of a new client. The chase and proving her talent were her favorite parts of the job. Her record was impeccable when it came to landing the premier accounts. She wasn't going to give this millionaire rancher the opportunity to consider any other agency to promote his new business, free-range beef.

The pilot tapped her on the shoulder and motioned that they were going to land.

"I'm ready," she called and drew a calming breath. This might be partly a vacation, but she planned to work her tail off too. It was the only thing she knew how to do. Besides, what else was there to do in Wyoming?

Waiting for the plane to land, Mitch Tucker leaned against his black Range Rover. His kids stood beside him at the end of the private landing strip. He was still wondering if he'd needed his head examined to agree to contact a New York ad agency. He'd relinquished that part of his life two years ago when he'd sold off all his international holdings. His focus was on business close to home in Wyoming. He'd resisted getting involved again with that old fast-paced lifestyle. He'd hoped to do everything locally, while being hands-on with the whole operation.

He glanced at his eleven-year-old daughter. Greta Caroline not only looked like her mother, blonde and fair-skinned with rich sapphire-blue eyes, she was also just as stubborn when she wanted something. His daughter was the one who'd practically taken over his idea to raise free-range beef.

Greta had spent hours on the Internet researching

marketing agencies for this project. And after he'd done some of his own research he knew they needed the right promotion to make their venture profitable. Not that he needed to worry about money. Working together with his kids was what mattered most. This was the first thing Greta had taken an interest in since her mother's death. He couldn't deny her this.

If it hadn't been for his children, losing Carrie would have finished him. At the time of their mother's death, Greta was nine and Colby was only three. Someone had to take care of them. That alone made Mitch drag himself out of bed every day, put one foot in front of the other and keep moving forward.

Two years later, he'd long since stopped his travel and gotten more involved in the ranching operation. But always in the center of everything were his kids. They were the reason he was standing here waiting for a New York executive to help promote his new beef program. This was just the beginning of his new life. Someday, he wanted to give his kids a complete family again.

"Please, Daddy, promise you'll be nice."

He looked down at his daughter's worried face. "This is business; you can't always be nice. I'll be polite."

"But you can be…intimidating."

"In business, that's not a bad way to be, Greta."

She sighed dramatically. "You said you'd give this a chance. I've researched this, and we need the right kind of advertising, the right market to promote our beef. Please, just listen to Ms Valentine's ideas."

He forced a smile. "I said I would, and you know I don't go back on my promises." *How in the hell is a New Yorker going to know anything about ranching in Wyoming?* "I talked with Brent Pierce and he's assured me that Ms Valentine is the right person for this job."

Greta nodded enthusiastically. "Rebecca Valentine is one of their top agents and a junior partner. She's worked for the Pierce Agency since college when she graduated Summa Cum Laude ten years ago—"

"Whoa, where did you get all this information?"

She looked up at him, showing off the pretty smile that was going to do him in. "I did my research like you taught me."

Before he could say anything more, Colby began jumping up and down, pointing to the other end of the runway as the plane touched down. "They're here, Dad."

When the plane stopped taxiing, Mitch took his son's hand and the three of them hurried onto the runway. He would give this a chance, just as he'd promised, realizing he had to be crazy to invite a career-driven female into his home. Ms Valentine wasn't the type of woman he planned to expose his kids to, or the type who would be content living on a cattle ranch.

Mitch paused next to the Cessna as his pilot and his ranch manager, Wally Hagan, walked around and popped open the passenger door. The first thing he saw of the New York agent was a pair of black high-heeled shoes that were attached to long, shapely legs. A sudden dryness in Mitch's throat made it difficult to swallow when bare knees and part of a thigh made an appearance.

Holding Wally's hand, the passenger finally made it out of the plane. Clearing the wing, she stepped into the sunlight and Mitch couldn't catch his breath. Rebecca Valentine was a tall woman with golden brown hair that was drawn back into a bun, except for a few wayward curls that circled her pretty face.

A smile touched her full mouth, but it was her light blue, almost gray eyes that he was drawn to. He didn't realize he'd been staring until his daughter nudged him.

"Ms Valentine…I'm Mitch Tucker," he said and held out his hand. "Welcome to Wyoming."

She had a firm handshake. "Please, call me Rebecca."

"And I'm Mitch." He quickly moved on. "This is my daughter, Greta."

She took the girl's hand. "Greta, it's good to finally meet you."

"I'm glad to meet you, too, Ms Valentine."

"Since we'll *all* be working together, please call me Rebecca."

Greta turned to her father and he nodded his permission.

Mitch gathered his small son in front of him. The five-year-old was already dirty and his dark curly hair unruly. "And this is Colby."

She leaned down to look in his eyes. "Hello, Colby."

Colby smiled, showing off his missing bottom tooth. "Hi, Rebecca, I'm five." He held up his spread fingers.

"My, that's old," she said. "I bet you go to school."

He bobbed his head. "This year I start kindergarten."

Mitch motioned to the SUV. "Well, let's take you to the house and get you settled in."

Wally helped Mitch load the suitcases and the kids climbed in back. He came around the passenger side to find Rebecca attempting to climb into the high seat. Her narrow skirt rose up dangerously, threatening Rebecca's modesty, and Mitch's sanity.

"SUVs and short skirts don't mix," she said. "I guess I didn't think about this outfit being impractical. I should have worn pants."

"Jeans might even be better," he offered. "If you'll allow me to help, we can get going."

"Sure."

She gasped as he scooped her up. He dropped her in the bucket seat, but not before he caught a whiff of her scent, and felt the enticing curve of her small waist.

"Like I said, pants will make it easier…for all of us." He grimaced, knowing his words were too revealing.

Hell, he'd been widowed for two years. Just about anything would set him off.

The house was even more impressive close up. Rebecca eyed the small details of the fence and flowers that hung from the front porch. Mitch pulled the car into the circular drive and continued around the structure to the back.

"We live pretty simply here and the back door is closer to everything," Mitch told her.

"I know," Rebecca replied. "I spent a lot of time at my grandparents', we always used the back door."

For some reason she was just chattering away. She knew Mitch Tucker hadn't been exactly thrilled about calling in a New York company, but a good businessman should want the right promotion for his product. She just needed to convince him that she was the best person to do that for him.

Once parked, she opened the truck door and got out without any help. Mitch grabbed her bags and went up the step to the small back porch. Colorful pots filled with flowers were arranged against the house, making the place look homely and welcoming.

Mitch opened the glass-paneled door and motioned her in. She walked into a mud room with a washer and dryer; several pairs of boots were lined against one wall. She crossed another threshold into a bright yellow kitchen with maple cabinets and white-tiled counters. A trestle-table sat in front of a row of windows that overlooked a view of the ranch.

"This is lovely," she said as Mitch walked through, carrying her bags down a hall.

She started to follow him when Greta stopped her. "Yellow was my mom's favorite color," the girl said.

Colby pulled a chair out and climbed up on it. "She died when I was really little," he announced as his brown eyes glistened.

"I'm sorry." Even though Rebecca knew the Tucker family history, she wasn't prepared to deal with this. No child should have to be without a mother.

"She loved us a whole bunch," the boy added.

"I'm sure she did," Rebecca said, fighting the urge to wrap her arms around this child.

"Do you have any little boys?" Colby asked.

Her chest tightened with the familiar pain. "No, I don't."

"Any little girls?"

Rebecca swallowed. Unable to speak, she shook her head.

Greta stepped in. "Colby, Rebecca is a career woman and she flies all over the country for her job."

Colby put his hands on his hips. "I know that, but she can have kids, too."

Mitch returned. "Hey, can't you two at least stop arguing until Rebecca gets settled? You don't want to scare her off."

The children's eyes widened. "We're sorry, Rebecca," Greta said.

Mitch pointed to the hall. "Why don't I show you to your room so you can rest?"

Rebecca was tired and her stomach was a little unsettled after the long trip into Denver, and the flight to the ranch. "How about I rest a while, then later we'll discuss some ideas?"

"You rest today. Tomorrow is soon enough," Mitch said.

Before Rebecca could argue, he was escorting her down the hall. He led her to a doorway off the main floor and opened double doors leading into a large bedroom. The walls were painted a pale blue with white crown moldings and off-white carpeting. A mahogany four-poster bed was adorned with an ecru satin comforter.

"Oh, this is a beautiful room." She sighed. "I think it's bigger than my entire apartment back in New York."

He smiled and she felt the jolt all the way to her toes. "Land is more plentiful here and I hope it stays that way." He waved to the full-sized bathroom. "There should be plenty of towels in the cabinet. If there's anything else you need let me know. Our housekeeper, Margie, is away for a few months on family business. So the kids and I are handling things on our own this summer."

"You are a brave man," Rebecca said without thinking.

His piercing brown eyes held hers, and he folded his arms against his broad chest. The man was big and gorgeous with thick, wavy dark brown hair. She couldn't help but enjoy the total package. Her gaze swept over the blue Western-cut shirt tucked into the narrow waist of his fitted dark denim jeans and on to his feet encased in snakeskin boots.

He could be an ad as the perfect cowboy.

"Are you saying I can't handle a hundred and forty sections of cattle ranch, a horse-breeding business, and two kids?"

Rebecca raised an eyebrow. "If your kids were just run-of-the-mill kids, but those two…" She nodded toward the kitchen. "They're scheming for a takeover."

That brought a wide, sexy grin. "You could be right." He took a step toward her. "So tell me, Rebecca Valentine, are you here to join forces with them, or save me?"

* * *

Two hours later, Mitch moved around the kitchen preparing an early supper, admonishing himself for flirting with Rebecca Valentine. This was business, and no matter how attractive she was he couldn't mix the two. Not that he wanted to. No. Even though he was attracted to her, he'd be crazy to get mixed up with a New Yorker, a career woman. No, this wasn't the woman he needed…

Mitch ran his hand over his face in frustration. He'd better get it together because she was going to be here a while, right under his roof. He just needed to think about what was good for Greta and Colby.

Okay, he could handle it. He went to the oven and checked on the enchiladas. Thanks to Margie, they had several prepared dishes in the freezer.

Margie Kline had been working for the Tuckers part-time since Colby was born. Then after Carrie's death, the widowed grandmother moved in to stay. She'd become a part of the family, and helped Mitch keep his sanity.

So when Margie had asked for a few months to stay with her sister during her hip surgery and recuperation, he hadn't been able to turn his housekeeper down. Besides, it gave him more time to spend with the kids. Of course, now he had a house guest.

Rebecca Valentine could stay in town, but he'd spend too much time driving her back and forth. This seemed to be the best solution, especially since he was needed here and she had to familiarize herself with the operation.

Greta came in and immediately began to take the dishes from the cupboard and set the table. "Do you think we should eat in the dining room? We have a guest."

"No, Greta. Rebecca is here to learn how we do things. She's going to get dirty just like the rest of us." Did she have clothes to wear on a ranch? Visions of her trying to get around in a short skirt had his body suddenly stirring to life.

"Is there anything I can do to help?"

Mitch glanced up to see Rebecca standing in the doorway. She had changed into a pair of gray pleated trousers and a wine-colored, short-sleeve blouse. She looked a lot shorter in her flat shoes, but that didn't take away from her appeal.

"Sure, you can pour the milk for the kids and iced tea for us," he told her. "It's in the refrigerator."

Rebecca went to the cupboard and found glasses. "Something smells wonderful."

"Enchiladas," Greta said.

"Did you make them?" she asked.

Greta smiled. "No, I can cook some things but these are Margie's specialty. She left us a lot of food in the freezer."

"We won't starve," Mitch said.

"I'm not worried," she told him. "Give me some lettuce and tomatoes and I'm happy."

He stopped opening the tortillas. "Please, don't tell me you're a vegetarian."

Rebecca enjoyed seeing the panicked look on Mitch Tucker's face. "No, I'm not. If I could I'd eat steak and burgers all the time. I just have to watch my weight."

She felt his intense gaze roam from her head down to her toes, spreading heat in its wake. She had never been able to obtain that lean look that was so popular. Rachel had gotten all the thin genes.

"You look fine," he told her.

"Those great-smelling enchiladas aren't going to help," she said as she took the milk and pitcher of iced tea from the refrigerator and placed them on the table.

Mitch put on oven mitts, took out the covered baking dish, and brought it to the table. Just then Colby raced into the room and jumped into his seat.

"Oh, boy," he cried, looking hungrily at the food.

"Did you wash your hands?"

A pair of big brown eyes widened as if deciding what to say. "I did this morning."

Mitch frowned and pointed to the door. "Go and wash."

"Okay." Colby got up.

"I should go with you," Rebecca said. "I forgot to wash mine, too. Will you show me the way?"

Colby perked up. "Sure. Come on. I have this cool soap that foams up and smells like bubble gum."

"Wow. I've got to see this." She glanced over her shoulder. "We'll be back shortly."

It wasn't long before there was laughter coming from the bathroom. There was nothing sweeter to Mitch's ears.

Finally the twosome returned and sat down at the table. Soon both his children were vying for Rebecca's attention. Mitch decided it wasn't that odd. Besides Margie there hadn't been many women in the house since their mother's death.

"Hey, Dad," Colby called. "Did you know that Rebecca knows how to ride? Her grandpa owned horses."

"Is that so?" he said, somewhat surprised. "Where was their farm?" He dished out a helping of enchiladas and handed it to her, then filled Colby's plate.

"Outside of Lexington, Virginia," Rebecca said. "My grandfather bred and trained Quarter Horses and European Warmbloods, all disciplines—hunters, jumpers and dressage. It was a small operation."

Mitch finished serving everyone. "Did your family move to New York?"

Family? That was something she'd never had. Not unless you counted the mismatched union her parents had called a marriage. "No, just my mother and sister; my parents divorced when I was pretty young."

For all their sakes, Robert and Diana Valentine had called it quits after a few years, but the bitterness had continued until her mother's death a decade ago. It also had caused their twin daughters to choose sides. That was how Rachel had ended up in the UK with their father, and Rebecca living in the States with their mother.

"Our mother moved us to Long Island to work. But I spent summers in Virginia, but once I started college it was too difficult to get back. And by then Poppy Crawford retired and sold the horse farm."

Mitch checked to see that Colby was eating, and took a bit himself. "You and your sister didn't want to follow family tradition?"

"My sister now resides with my father's family," she said, recalling since their mother's death just how many years it had been since she'd seen Rachel. Along with her other family members, Grandfather William, her father, half-brothers and -sisters.

"She works in London. Our father is British."

"Wow! Do you go to London?" Greta asked.

"I haven't been back there in years."

Rebecca wondered how they'd sidetracked her. She wasn't used to revealing so much family history. There was only one person she'd ever shared the Valentines' sins with; her friend, Stephanie Ellison.

"These enchiladas are great," she said. "Margie is a great cook."

Mitch must have seen her discomfort. "Kids, why don't you finish eating? You have other chores."

They groaned.

"All right, if they don't get done today, then you can't ride out to see the herd tomorrow."

"Okay," Greta said. After they cleaned their plates Colby helped his sister carry their plates to the sink.

Once they were out of earshot, Mitch turned back to Rebecca. "I apologize for all the questions."

"They're curious."

"Do you think you can handle them for the next few weeks?"

The kids weren't going to be her problem. Rebecca smiled. "One thing about kids: they're open and honest for the most part. I find that refreshing."

"It can get stale pretty quick." He turned serious. "If you ever feel they're infringing on your privacy, just let me know."

She laughed. "As big as this house is, I can't believe we'll get in each other's way. Besides, it's very gracious of you to invite me to stay here."

He got up and took down two mugs from the cupboard. "Coffee?"

At her nod, he did his task. As he walked back to the table she couldn't help but be aware of his powerful presence—but at the same time how comfortable he seemed waiting on her.

"This is a pretty rural area. One of the reasons I

have my own plane is to get in and out fast. The winters can be treacherous."

"They can be in New York, too." She took a sip of coffee. The kids were on the other side of the kitchen doing dishes, chatting away. A good-looking man was sitting across from her as they shared coffee.

Yes, she used to see herself in this life with a man and children. Now…

"Rebecca…"

She turned toward Mitch's voice. "Sorry," she said, embarrassed. "I guess I drifted off."

"I'd say it's more likely jet lag. You've flown a long way. I doubt you slept much in the last twenty-four hours."

"If you don't mind, I think I will call it a day."

"I don't mind at all," he told her. "I want you rested when we ride out tomorrow. There's a lot to see."

It just dawned on her that she'd probably landed this account because she was the only one in the firm that could ride a horse. Was this all-too-good-looking cowboy waiting to see if she could keep up? She'd been crazy to think she could relax.

"I'll be ready."

CHAPTER TWO

REBECCA woke up to a soft knock at her door. She rolled over in the big bed, fighting sleep.

"Rebecca," a man's muffled voice came through the closed door.

Mitch. She sat up, trying to clear her head. "Just a minute," she called as she threw the blanket back and grabbed her robe off the end of the bed. She walked to the door, jabbing her arms through the sleeves. Belt tied, she ran her hand over her hair to tame the wild curls and opened the door.

There stood Mitch Tucker, dressed in a pressed tan Western shirt and a pair of faded jeans. He had a smile on his clean-shaven face, not looking the least bit apologetic for waking her at this ungodly hour.

"I'm sorry, did I oversleep?" she asked, looking over her shoulder at the darkness outside her window.

"I didn't really give you a specific time." He

leaned against the doorjamb. "It's six and we usually have breakfast at six-thirty. Can you make it?"

"Sure," she lied. "That'll give me plenty of time."

He nodded, but didn't move to leave. "Are you sure you're up for riding today?" His voice was husky and low, causing a shiver along her spine.

She could only manage to nod.

"We could get there in the four-by-four."

She was touched by his concern. "No need. I can ride, but just take into account that I haven't ridden in years."

He smiled, and Rebecca couldn't breathe. "You should be fine," he assured her. "Besides, we'll have Colby and Greta with us so there's no rush. I thought I'd pack some sandwiches for lunch, make an easy day of it. There's a lot of pretty country to see. It might give you some ideas on the marketing campaign."

"I'll be sure to take my notepad."

All at once Rebecca was too aware of the cozy silence in the house, and the gorgeous man standing just outside her bedroom. How was she supposed to concentrate on business?

"Do you have some jeans and a pair of boots?" he asked.

"I brought some. So…I'd better get in the shower if you want me ready on time."

"And I'll go start breakfast."

"Bye," she said and closed the door. *Great, I come to Wyoming and let a man distract me.*

Over the years, she had perfected the "this is strictly business" look when it came to clients wanting more from her—not that Mitch wanted more from her. But whenever the man came near her, she wasn't sure she knew her own name. Worse, thirty seconds ago, she hadn't cared.

"Well, you better care," Rebecca scolded herself. She yanked fresh underwear and a pair of jeans from the drawer, then a blouse from the closet. She headed for the tumbled-stone-tiled bathroom, and turned on the shower.

Somehow she had to regain her footing on this, or she was in big trouble. This was her career. She couldn't mess this up.

It was all she had left.

At six-thirty on the dot, Rebecca walked into the kitchen. Mitch couldn't help but stare. He wasn't sure he'd seen a woman in a pair of jeans look so good…so sexy. A white oxford-cloth blouse was tucked into her small waist. But it was her hair pulled back with clips, hanging free and curled against her shoulders, that had him blink.

"Good morning," he said to her.

"It will be as soon as I find some coffee," she said and walked toward the pot.

"Help yourself," he told her as he removed the rest of the bacon from the skillet and placed it on a paper towel. "How do you like your eggs?"

"However you're having them." She gulped some caffeine and her expression changed to immediate pleasure.

It made him wonder what else pleased her, causing a jolt to his body. He quickly diverted those thoughts. "Have a seat."

"No, I'll help you." She took another sip and set her mug on the table, then went to the cupboard and found the plates, arranging four place settings at the table. "Where are Greta and Colby?"

"They're still asleep." He leaned against the counter. "A parent needs some quiet time."

"So that's your secret."

He glanced out the window toward the rising sun. "Early morning was always when Carrie and I got to spend time together, especially since I traveled so much back then. I guess I still like it."

"You shouldn't feel as if you had to invite me for breakfast if you'd rather be alone."

"I didn't." He was too aware of her. "I wanted to share breakfast with you," he said, then rushed on to say, "I mean…maybe we could run over some ideas without…interruptions."

She blinked and nodded. "Sure. If that's what you want."

What he wanted could get him into trouble. "Why don't we enjoy the peace and quiet first?"

The moment ended with a thundering sound on the stairs. They smiled. "I guess that was wishful thinking."

"Dad, Colby didn't make his bed," Greta announced as she walked in.

"I did, too," the boy argued. "It's just not made her way."

"Greta, Colby," he said. "Remember your manners."

Both children mumbled their good mornings.

"Now, sit down before you drive Rebecca back to New York."

The children took their seats. "Sorry, Rebecca," Greta said.

"Yeah, sorry, Rebecca," Colby repeated. "I hope you stay with us."

"I'd like to," she told them. "I wouldn't want to miss the ride today."

Their eyes widened. "Are we going for sure?" Greta asked.

Mitch glanced over his shoulder giving them both his best stern look. "I'm still thinking about it." He turned back and poured eggs into the skillet.

That was when he heard Colby whisper, "That means yes."

Over the next hour, Rebecca helped pack sandwiches and drinks. Then everyone headed out the door toward one of the barns. She couldn't help but be impressed by the obviously well-run ranch. There were several ranch hands at work doing their assigned chores.

Wally and another young man had four horses saddled and waiting for them next to the barn. Suddenly Rebecca was both excited and fearful.

The forty-something ranch manager tipped his hat. "Good morning, Rebecca."

"Good morning, Wally," she returned the greeting. "Are you going with us?"

"No, ma'am," he said with a smile, causing tiny lines to crinkle around his hazel eyes. "I'm sorry to say I have work to do." He glanced at Mitch. "You enjoy yourself, though. It's a pretty ride. And you'll have a great mount here with Ginger."

"Dad, Rebecca's going to ride Ginger?" Greta asked.

Mitch exchanged a glance with Wally. "I thought she'd be the best mount for her." He went to the chestnut mare and patted her neck. "You can trust her; she's gentle," he assured her.

"Mom used to ride her," Colby said.

Rebecca felt odd. How could she ride Carrie Tucker's horse? "Are you sure?"

"Ginger, here, is getting a little stocky." The horse shifted at Mitch's insult and everyone laughed. "The ride today will do her good."

"This is my horse, Rebecca." Greta went to a

small Appaloosa mare, brown with a sprinkling of small white snowflake-like spots. "Her name is Snow Princess. Dad gave her to me for my birthday."

"That's quite a present."

As if not to be outdone, Colby spoke up. "When I'm ten, Dad says I can have my own horse, too. Right now, I'm riding Trudy." His mount was a small bay mare. Rebecca knew enough about horses to recognize that this mare had been around for many years. She was as docile as a family pet.

"Dad's got the best horse, White Knight," the boy said.

Rebecca's gaze went to the impressive stallion, a white Appaloosa with four black stockings, mane and tail. This animal was the most spirited.

She was drawn to the beautiful beast. She knew about Mitch's Appaloosa breeding program. "Is he one of your studs?"

"Not much any more." Mitch patted the horse's neck and the animal bobbed his head and whinnied. "His male offspring have taken over for the most part. If you're interested, I can show you around my breeding operation."

Keep focused on business. "If you have time," she said and went back to her horse while Mitch assisted his kids up on their horses.

"Need some help?" he called to her.

"Not unless the way you mount a horse is different now than when I was a kid," she said teasingly as she tugged the borrowed straw cowboy hat lower on her forehead. She took the reins, put her foot in the stirrup and began to pull herself up when she felt Mitch's hands on her waist. She bit back a gasp as he helped and lifted her into the saddle.

"I could have managed."

"Just thought I'd help," he said with a wink. "How do the stirrups feel?"

"They're a little long," she told him.

Mitch immediately adjusted one, then the other. "How's that?" he asked. His hand on her leg was more disturbing than she'd like.

"It's fine." Rebecca backed away, putting the unfamiliar horse through a few basic commands. She was pleasantly surprised at the easy ride.

Mitch nodded when she finished, then he strolled to his horse. His easy gait let her know he was comfortable in this element. And he had a great-looking backside in a pair of jeans. She watched as he took the reins and swung his leg over the horse's back into the saddle.

"Let's go." He turned and started across the yard to the gate. A ranch hand held it open until they went through. The four of them ambled along the trail in pairs, Colby and Mitch, followed by Greta and Rebecca.

Although it was May, the morning sun promised

to heat up the day soon enough. And with a three-mile ride, it was going to take some time.

Before long Rebecca got into a rhythm with her horse. She leaned back and began to enjoy the ride.

Greta was quite the tour guide, pointing out landmarks. The Rocky Mountains made a proud backdrop against the rich blue sky, white billowy clouds scattered around as if in a painting. Rows of aspen trees moved with the gentle breeze.

"You should see the aspens in the fall. The leaves turn bright gold and red," Greta explained as she pointed toward the mountains. "And see the pine trees? At Christmas we get to go up there and find a really big tree and cut it down. That was my mom's favorite time of year."

"Mine, too," Rebecca said. "I love New York at Christmas time with all the lights and decorations." She also remembered an earlier time as a child in England with her mother and her father…and sister. She thought about her grandfather William. What was he now—ninety? As a child, he'd always smiled and hugged her a lot. Even though those holidays had been stiff and formal in William's London home, they meant family to Rebecca. Besides the grandchildren had always been able to escape upstairs where there had been a special room loaded with books and toys.

She smiled. "It's good to have memories."

"Hey, you two," Mitch called. "Try and keep up."

"Yeah, try and keep up," Colby echoed his father.

"He's such a brat," Greta said.

Rebecca smiled again. "One day, when you grow up, the two of you can be good friends. Just don't lose touch with the people you love."

The young girl looked concerned. "Did you lose touch with your sister? Is it because England is so far away?"

"That's one of the reasons," Rebecca admitted. "But even being twins, we were very different."

"You're a twin." Her companion's blue eyes widened. "What's her name?"

"Rachel."

"Rachel and Rebecca," Greta said. "That's so cool. Does anyone ever call you Becca?"

Emotions rushed through Rebecca as she remembered her dad's pet name for her. "Someone did once. A long time ago."

Rebecca couldn't help but smile. Her body actually began to relax. She could get used to this. It might be the best medicine for what ailed her. Well, that wasn't quite true, but it was a start.

Mitch tried to keep an eye on Rebecca to see how she was handling the ride. Maybe he should have driven them up here to see the herd. Three miles wasn't far if you were used to being on horseback. This New Yorker wasn't.

He dropped off the trail and waited for Greta and Rebecca to catch up. "Greta, go ride with your brother for a while."

"Okay, Dad, but he better mind me."

"There's no reason to boss him. Just stay on the trail and I'll be back in a few minutes." He patted the horse's rump and Princess moved up to Colby's mount.

Mitch fell in beside Rebecca. "How are you holding up?"

"Pretty good, but I have a feeling that I'll know better tomorrow." She shifted in the saddle. "Please don't worry about me. I'm truly enjoying the ride. I haven't seen this much open land in years. You have a gorgeous ranch, Mr Tucker."

"I know." He smiled as he glanced around. "It's not everyone's taste, but it is mine. Feel free to enjoy." His gaze settled on her. He liked her hair down. Made her look younger, more relaxed, as if she belonged here. But she didn't. "We'll be in the valley in another mile."

"No hurry," she assured him.

Mitch didn't switch places with Greta. He was enjoying the view right where he was. He couldn't help but watch Rebecca. She sat on a horse with ease and grace, but she was also in control.

"Did you train horses with your grandfather?"

She smiled. "If you mean exercise them, and muck

out stalls, yes. Poppy said I had to earn my way up. By the time I was old enough, my time there was limited. But, yes, I did get to help some. I rode jumpers. Believe me, I've fallen off my share of horses."

"That's better than getting bucked off. I spent some time trying to rodeo. Decided I could find easier ways to earn money."

Rebecca laughed and he found he liked the sound. They rode for a while in silence before Mitch asked, "Do you miss being around horses?" He stole a glance at her. "I mean, I've done a lot of business in New York—the pace can be grueling."

She sighed. "I agree, but I need to be in New York for my line of work. I've gotten used to the pace and madness."

"I guess you're right," he conceded. "I just noticed how relaxed you look right now."

"I can relax in New York, too," she said.

He started to disagree when Greta called to him. They reached their destination. In the clearing was a large grassy valley surrounded by a barbed-wire fence.

"Welcome to Freedom Valley. It's fenced in to keep the cattle in the pasture that's free of any pesticides." He directed the riders up along the fence.

"The herd consists of over a hundred and fifty head of Angus mix," he told her, and remembered that this was supposed to be a new beginning for his family. He'd been planning and preparing this project for quite a while.

"This isn't exactly a new way to raise cattle. It's going back to the old way of free-range beef."

"They don't look any different," Rebecca said.

"But they're being raised differently. They're fed for eighteen months on only grass, then they're transferred to feed lots and grain-fed for another hundred and twenty days. No hormones, antibiotics, pesticides, or animal products."

"I guess, for a steer, it can't get any better than that."

They continued to ride and came up to one of the Angus calves. A black-faced yearling made a bawling sound at them. Greta pointed. "Look, Dad, it's Blackie. He remembers me."

"Greta, you know you don't name cattle. They aren't pets."

"He's the only one, only because he got tangled up in the fence and we had to call the vet. Remember I got to take care of him for a few days."

Mitch looked at Rebecca. "I know it sounds cruel, but it's better for the kids, rather than have them cry their eyes out when the animals go off to the slaughterhouse."

"I'm not disagreeing with you," she said and glanced at the calf. "But look at that face…"

Mitch groaned, but he was finding he enjoyed their easy banter too much. "Okay, who wants lunch?"

Rebecca was too lazy, but she'd get up just as soon as she gathered the strength. Lying on a blanket under the shade of trees, next to a trickling stream, was only something written about in books. Places like this weren't real life.

"Rebecca, are you asleep?" Colby asked.

She opened her eyes. "No, of course not. I'm just resting my eyes." She sat up and smiled at the boy. He had peanut butter on his cheek and his shirt was dirty. He was adorable.

"That's what Dad is doing, too."

She glanced at the man stretched out on his back on the other side of the blanket. His legs were crossed at the ankle, hands folded on his chest, and his hat covered his face. "Well, he works hard. He deserves some rest."

Colby leaned close to her and whispered, "I think he's playin' possum. He's not really asleep." The boy's hand was over his mouth to hold back a giggle. He leaned closer to his father. Suddenly Mitch reached out, grabbed the child by his waist and wrestled him to the ground.

Colby laughed and finally cried out, "Uncle! Uncle!"

His father released him. "That will teach you to

sneak up on a cowboy." He ruffled his son's hair and grinned at Rebecca. His own hair was messy, his dark eyes piercing into hers.

"Did you get enough to eat?"

"More than," she said and grabbed her backpack. "I was thinking maybe we should have an impromptu meeting."

Mitch lay on his side and propped his head up on his hand and turned those deep-set brown eyes on Rebecca. Colby sat down beside her, and Greta was next to her father.

"Okay," Mitch said.

Suddenly she wasn't so sure of herself. "I was thinking that we should have a company slogan for your website."

"I think we should use our family name," Greta said. "People know it." The young girl looked at her father. "I mean, Great-Grandpa and Grandpa Tucker have raised cattle in Wyoming for a long time. That should mean something to people."

"That's good, Greta," Rebecca encouraged. "People like and trust family-run businesses." She jotted it down, eager to prove her worth to Mitch Tucker and that she was prepared for this job. "My assistant in New York is working on a nationwide list of specialty grocery stores that carry free-range meats." She smiled. "Even I was surprised how many there are, or how in demand free-range beef is. I'll have the list for you in a few days." She looked down at her notes. "I understand that you're going to be processing your own beef."

Mitch nodded, and reached over to put his hand on her tablet so she couldn't look at any more notes. "How about we renew this discussion tomorrow at the meeting?"

Rebecca recognized his determination. And she liked the challenge of this project. It was hard for her to stop when she got started on something, but he was the boss. She nodded. "Sure. Tomorrow."

He moved his hand. "I have no doubt you're good at your job, but we got to take time to relax."

"I don't have trouble relaxing, it's just not when I'm working."

"I don't do business the usual way any more. I'm not on deadline." He smiled at Greta and Colby. "Not any more. Right, kids?"

"Right, Dad," they said in unison, then turned to her.

She'd be the first to admit she didn't take time for herself, and this trip to Wyoming had been supposed to be part vacation. But she was never good at relaxing, especially when she started a new project.

"Come on, Rebecca," Mitch began. "It's a great afternoon, enjoy it."

"Yeah, Rebecca," Colby said as he stretched out beside his dad.

Mitch pointed toward her notebook. "Here's something you can write down," he told her as he rolled on his back, but his gaze didn't leave her face. "I'm going to have to teach you how we do things in Wyoming. First thing is how to enjoy a lazy afternoon."

CHAPTER THREE

"Okay, son, we're home," Mitch said.

Colby didn't fight him as the boy slid out of the saddle into his dad's waiting arms. "We had fun."

"We sure did," he said as the child dropped his head against his shoulder. "Maybe we should rest."

"I'm five...I don't take naps any more," Colby murmured.

"I know, but maybe we can just lie down for a while."

Greta climbed off Princess. She also looked a little fatigued. "I feel fine, Dad."

"And you did great today, sweetheart. Thanks for all your help."

"Rebecca did great, too," his daughter said. "She's a good rider."

Mitch looked toward the last mount. Wally took hold of Ginger's reins as Rebecca climbed down. He didn't miss the grimace on her face, but she quickly put on a smile when Wally said something to her. "Yes, she is." He hadn't found much about Rebecca Valentine that she couldn't do. "Let's head up to the house and out of the heat."

Rebecca walked toward them carrying the backpack. "Looks like we lost one," she said, reaching out to push away the dark hair off Colby's forehead.

"He held up better than I expected." He shifted his son a little higher. "Let's go up to the house. This guy is heavy."

Rebecca handed the backpack to Greta. "If you wouldn't mind, I'd like to take care of Ginger. It's been a while since I've groomed a horse."

Mitch frowned. "Are you sure?"

Rebecca nodded. "You said I could have the rest of the day off."

Before he could say anything, his daughter appeared.

"Dad, can I stay and help, too?" Greta asked. "I mean, I should take care of my own horse."

Wally came up to the group. "Not to worry, Mitch. I'll take care of the ladies."

"I'm sure you will," Mitch said. Not having a choice, he headed off toward the house.

Wally Hagan was more than just Mitch's ranch manager and his pilot. Divorced for years, he'd worked for the Tucker ranch for years. Wally had watched over Mitch's family as if they were his own, and he'd been the one who called him about Carrie's automobile accident. He had flown to get him so he could see his wife in the end.

Wally was a good man. He'd known him to have an easy smile and quite a way with the ladies.

Did he have his eye on Rebecca?

Mitch found himself feeling something he didn't like. Jealousy? How could that be? The last thing he needed was to get involved with a career woman.

After Rebecca finished with Ginger, she made it back to the house, showered and changed into clean clothes. She braided her damp hair and left her bedroom in search of Mitch. She'd had second thoughts about not working the afternoon.

She came down the hall, but instead of going into the kitchen she wandered into the great room. The high ceilings, along with the huge brick fireplace, made it look bigger than it was. The hardwood floors glistened with high polish. There was a big-screen television, a cocoa-colored leather sofa and two matching overstuffed chairs. Oval patterned rugs covered the seating area. In the corner sat an overflowing toy box. This was definitely a family-friendly room.

She went into the front hall and found a carved oak staircase that curved upward and around the open second-story hall. A cut-glass chandelier hung over a round antique pedestal table in the center of the marble floor. She glanced into a parlor that had more of a feminine touch with the Victorian-style furniture. Over a tiled fireplace hung a portrait of the Tucker family that drew her in for a closer look.

Mitch looked handsome and a little younger in his dark Western suit. The beautiful blonde next to him had to be his wife, Carrie Tucker. She was a slender woman with startling blue eyes and a warm smile. On her lap she held a dark-haired toddler. Rebecca couldn't help but smile at the cute Colby. In between her parents was a younger Greta with her curly blonde hair and light eyes that were so much like her mother's.

The perfect family.

A feeling of envy came over Rebecca. The Tucker family represented everything Rebecca wanted and couldn't have—a man like Mitch and…children.

She turned and walked out. Passing Mitch's study, she paused, hearing movement behind the closed door. Suddenly she wasn't in the mood to talk business. She kept walking until she reached the louvered doors that led into a sun room.

The late-afternoon sun shone through the row of windows and Rebecca took a seat on the padded bench below and stared out at the mountains.

She hadn't had a day like today in years, hadn't ridden since she was a teenager, and she wasn't half bad at it. With a proud smile, she relaxed back against the overstuffed cushions and closed her eyes. She stretched to relieve the stiffness in her back.

It wouldn't hurt to rest here for a minute, then get up and help Mitch with supper. Warmth spread through her as she thought about the combination sexy cowboy and dad. He was a pleasant surprise for her…too pleasant.

Mitch searched the house, but couldn't find Rebecca anywhere. He'd even called down to the barn, looking for her. Wally seemed amused that he couldn't locate his house guest.

Finally he peeked into the sun room. That was where she was, curled up on the bench. He watched her even breathing and knew she was sleeping. His gaze moved to her slightly parted lips, then to her hair, mussed just enough to look sexy. Man, a hundred things began to run through his head, none of which he wanted to analyze. Why did this woman get to him? The obvious answer was Rebecca Valentine was a beautiful woman.

In the twelve years he and Carrie had been married, he'd never looked at another woman. His wife had been everything to him. But it was so long since she died. So long…

He stole another glance at Rebecca as she slept peacefully. A long braid hung over her shoulder, and strands of curls clung to her cheek. She didn't have on any makeup, exposing tiny freckles across her nose. Otherwise, her skin was flawless.

Feeling his body stir, Mitch sank into the wicker chair across the room. What was he doing looking at this woman as if she were dessert? He knew better. She was running his campaign. If that weren't bad enough, she was staying in his home. If anything he should run in the other direction.

He started to get up when he heard her moan and shift again. She blinked her eyes and finally looked at him. "Oh, Mitch," she whispered hoarsely.

That got his heart beating even faster. "Sorry, I didn't mean to disturb you."

She sat up and pushed back her hair. "I must have fallen asleep. What time is it?"

"A little after five," he said, checking his watch. "You needed to rest after today." He nodded. "I must say you were a real trooper and pretty good on horseback."

"It was fun. As I said, it's been a while since I rode." Her smile widened. "It brought back memories of my sister and me going riding at the farm. Rachel was a natural, even did a little competive riding."

"You two were close?"

She shrugged. "We were until after college she wanted to return to the UK."

Mitch heard the sadness in her voice. Suddenly he made a connection with her name. "Would your grandfather happen to be William Valentine of the Bella Lucia restaurant?"

"Afraid so," she said.

"I can believe it. It's one of my favorite restaurants. Whenever I had business in London, I made sure that I dined there."

"My grandfather would be happy to hear that. And before you ask why I live and work in New York, and not London for the family business, let me say that our mother was American. And after my parents' divorce, Mom brought Rachel and me back to the States." She glanced away. "I never had much desire to go back to the UK, not like Rachel… She enjoys working with our father."

Mitch figured there was a lot more to this story. "Your sister went into the family business and you chose something else to do, and somewhere else to live. I'm sure your mother is happy that she has one of her daughters here," he said.

Once again Rebecca realized how easily this man got her to talk—about her family, no less. Why stop now? Her gaze locked with his. "Mother died about a year after we graduated college."

"I'm sorry. That's tough."

"She had been sick a long time. As they say, it was a blessing in the end."

Mitch's expression didn't give much away. "It's never a blessing for those who are left behind."

"I'm sorry, Mitch. I didn't mean to bring back memories…"

"You didn't bring them back; they're with me all the time." He patted the spot over his shirt pocket. "The kids had it bad for a long time. Hell, so did I. But we got through it." He drew a shaky breath. "If I've learned one thing from losing Carrie, it's never to take anyone or anything for granted. That is why this project is so important to me. I want to build something with Greta and Colby."

Rebecca swallowed back the lump in her throat. All she'd ever known were broken families. A father who'd never had time for her; a mother who had been bitter over a man. All men. But the love for his family shining in Mitch Tucker's eyes brought tears to hers.

He looked at her and a half-smile moved across that sexy mouth. "Now you know my secret."

She blinked. "What secret?"

"I'd rather watch a Disney movie with my kids than travel the world, or handle acquisitions in the boardroom."

She raised an eyebrow. "And what will you pay for my silence?"

He held her gaze a long time. "How about you go riding again…?"

"I'm listening," she said, realizing she could easily become hooked on the activity.

"I'll show you more of the ranch, but this time without the kids."

"Won't we be playing hookey?" It wasn't a good idea to get too personal with this man, but...

He leaned forward. "I bet you haven't had a vacation in years. And I can guess that your blood pressure is a little high. You drink too much caffeine and probably eat every lunch at your desk."

She gasped. "How—?"

"I used to be you," he said. "Everything I did was to build an empire. All the long days...and nights, I thought were so important, didn't mean squat in the end. If I had it to do all over again, I'd have a dozen more kids and stay right here on this ranch." He leaned back. "It took a while but I managed to slow down." His eyes brightened. "Kids will do that for you."

Of course he wanted more kids, Rebecca thought painfully. And he had that option. But what did she have besides work? "I still have a job to do."

"I know, but you don't have to live it twenty-four seven. Pace yourself. There's time. I'm paying your agency enough that you can afford to stay here for as long as it takes."

She couldn't stay here indefinitely. "What about my other clients?"

Darn the man if he didn't grin like a devil. She could see the tiny lines around his eyes, the only thing that gave away his age at forty-two. "Have you ever heard of delegating?"

"That's all well and good, but how would you feel if I delegated this job?"

He raised an eyebrow. "I thought Brent Pierce was going to handle my account, but he said you were the one for the job. I trusted him to know what was best." He nodded. "He did know, because he sent me you."

The way he'd said it, she felt as if she'd been awarded to him as a prize. *Don't dwell on those thoughts.* "I truly can't see Brent Pierce on Ginger." She giggled. Rebecca couldn't even picture the man out of his Hugo Boss suit. "Thank you for your confidence."

"I can't wait to hear your ideas."

"And we should get back at it bright and early tomorrow."

The sound of Greta's voice drew their attention.

"We're on the sun porch," Mitch called to her.

Both children appeared. Colby's face and hands were washed and he had on a clean shirt. Greta had probably had something to do with that.

"Hi, Dad and Rebecca," she said. "Dad, who's going to fix supper? I'm hungry."

"I'm doing it."

"That doesn't seem fair," Rebecca said, drawing all the Tucker family's attention. "Wouldn't it be easier if we took turns? We could make up teams. I'll partner with Greta, and Mitch, you partner with Colby. How does that sound?"

The three looked at each other, and Mitch said, "Rebecca, are you sure about this?"

She nodded. "You've all been gracious enough to open up your home to me. Please, I'd feel better if I help out some, especially since your housekeeper is away."

"Well, if it means that much to you," Mitch said, "then the kitchen is all yours."

She stood. "Okay, Greta, it's the girls against the guys. We'll take tonight."

"You're on, girls." Mitch gave his son a high five.

"We'll win, right, Dad," Colby said.

Rebecca placed her arm around Greta's shoulders. "Not when there's all this girl power." They turned and left the room, hearing the muffled words of a declared war behind them.

This was a war for Rebecca. A war to stay focused on her objective. She needed to win here, because she had to come to terms with what she was losing once she returned to New York.

"That was a great meal," Mitch said, tipping his chair back from the table.

"You know it was one of Margie's casseroles," Greta admitted. "But we made the salad and bread."

"Everything was delicious." He leaned across the

table and kissed her forehead. He looked at Rebecca. "You, too. It was nice to have a night off."

"For me, it's a pleasure to cook. I don't do it often. I can only make a few dishes. Cooking for one isn't much fun."

"What about your boyfriend?" Greta asked.

Mitch glanced at his daughter. "Rebecca's private life isn't our business."

"But, Dad, she knows all about us," Greta said, then turned back to Rebecca.

"I don't mind answering," she told him. "No, Greta, there isn't a special man in my life. Not that there haven't been a few over the years."

"Anyone famous?" Greta asked with growing interest.

This time Rebecca did smile. She looked young and carefree. "Well, I didn't date anyone famous, but I've met a few. Let's see… Oh, I went to a movie première for *Spiderman*."

Colby's eyes rounded. "Wow, you saw *Spiderman*?"

Rebecca nodded.

"Who else have you met?" Greta asked.

"There was Russell Crowe…Tom Hanks and Hilary Duff. Some Broadway stars you wouldn't know. A few New York Yankees—"

"The Yankees?" Mitch sat up. "Who?"

"Well, let's see, there was Derek Jeter and Gary Sheffield—oh, and Joe Torre."

"You've met Jeter and Sheffield?" he demanded.

She nodded. "That was a few years ago. Our firm did some PR work for a charitable organization."

"Your job is so cool." Greta pouted as she began to clear the table. "We *never* get to meet anyone famous here."

"I didn't at your age, either," Rebecca assured her as she got up and carried dishes to the sink.

Mitch watched the two together at the sink. Rebecca was talking to his daughter, soothing her sulky mood. Then finally the two began to laugh. Greta came back to the table to gather more dishes.

"Dad, do you want some coffee?"

"No, thank you." He stood. "Why don't you take Colby upstairs and start his bath? I'll finish the dishes."

She looked up at him and smiled. "Sure. Come on, Colby."

His son looked suspicious of his sister's sudden sweetness. "Can I play with my army men?"

Greta sighed. "Okay, but only for a little while." She took her brother's hand and they started out of the kitchen. Greta paused at the door. "Rebecca, thanks for going today. It was fun."

Rebecca smiled. "It was fun for me, too. Remember, tomorrow I want more of your input on this campaign. We'll work on it first thing."

"I'll see you in the morning." Greta tugged on Colby's arm and they left.

Mitch stood and brought glasses to the sink where Rebecca was rinsing them and placing them in the dishwasher.

"Okay, tell me what you said to Greta that made her laugh."

She shrugged. "Not much. We just talked. Adolescence is a rough time. You're not exactly a kid, but you're not quite a woman."

Mitch groaned. "Please, not my baby girl. I'm not ready for that change yet."

Rebecca would have given anything for this kind of concern from her father, but Robert Valentine hadn't had the time for her. "It'll happen sooner than you realize, so you'd better get ready. Greta is a beautiful girl. Before you know it she'll be dating—"

"They'll have to go through me first," Mitch insisted. "Teenage boys have one-track minds."

Rebecca bit back a smile. "I didn't know it was just teenage boys whose minds worked that way."

"I suppose we can all be jerks."

"Okay, I have to admit, I've met my share." She wouldn't put Mitch Tucker into that category. "Still, not all men are jerks."

He rewarded her with a crooked smile. "It's nice to know that a few of us are salvageable." He rested his hip against the counter and folded his arms across his broad chest. "What do you look for in a man?"

The question surprised her. It had been so long

since she'd taken time to date, she wasn't sure what she wanted in a man. "I guess the basics. No games. Honesty. Treats me with respect."

Mitch leaned in closer. "That should go without saying. You should try Wyoming men. They know how to treat a woman."

Was he flirting with her? Oh, brother, she was in bad shape if she didn't even know that. "Wyoming men, huh?"

"Of course, we live a slower pace here. We take time with…everything." He was so near she could feel his breath against her face, and his dark eyes were locked with hers.

"That would be nice," she managed to say. "I have to say, I haven't had much time to think about a relationship."

"That's a lonely existence," he said. "I know… sometimes…it's nice to have another person just to talk to." His gaze moved over her face, causing her heart to pound against her ribs.

"It would be nice to share your day with someone," she added.

He sighed. "Yeah, I think I miss that the most." His hand rose toward her face, then Greta called from the top of the stairs. Mitch pulled back. "I better go check on them."

"Go on, I'll finish up the kitchen," she told him. "Then I'm going to turn in."

After Mitch walked out, Rebecca finally let out a long breath. What was she doing? She was here on a job, not to audition for the role of the second Mrs Mitchell Tucker. She was going to get her heart broken if she wasn't careful.

She took the sponge and wiped off the counters. If she let herself, she could fall and fall hard. That wouldn't do. They had different plans for the future. She had her career. He was into kids, and she couldn't have any. With him or anyone else.

That painful truth was going to keep her on track.

CHAPTER FOUR

THE next morning, Mitch glanced at the kitchen clock. It was after seven, and Rebecca hadn't appeared for breakfast. He poured a second cup of coffee, knowing he had to leave soon.

The kids had gone into town with Jimmy to pick up some supplies so they were taken care of until about noon. That gave him the opportunity to handle business with Jake Peters at the breeding corral. Mitch's stallion, Kid Knight, was scheduled to cover Jake's mare, Dancer's Lady. But right now Mitch's mind wasn't only on equine breeding.

He recalled last night, and how he'd nearly stepped over the line. He always prided himself on being able to keep his business and his personal life separate. Now he'd brought one big temptation right here into his own home. And after only two days, he couldn't stop fantasizing about Rebecca.

Was she sore after yesterday's ride? He probably

should have offered her the use of his Jacuzzi tub last night. He drew in a quick breath. No. All he needed was to picture Rebecca Valentine naked in bubbling water and he'd never be able to go into his bathroom without thinking about her there.

Mitch took another sip of coffee and decided to leave her a note, then she walked into the kitchen. She was dressed in a pink tailored blouse and khaki slacks. Her hair was pulled back into a ponytail. Today, she looked as if she belonged on a ranch.

"Good morning."

She nodded and walked to the coffeemaker. He was ahead of her, poured a full mug, then handed it to her. After a few sips, she finally smiled. "Good morning." She glanced around the kitchen. "Where are Colby and Greta?"

"Jimmy took them into town on some errands." Mitch retrieved a covered plate from the stove and brought it to the table. "They'll be back in a few hours so enjoy the peace while you can."

"You didn't have to fix me breakfast." Rebecca wasn't used to people waiting on her. She looked at the scrambled eggs and sausage and realized she was hungry. "This is nice." She sat down and started to eat.

"Glad to see you have an appetite."

"I've always had an appetite."

"Well, after all the physical activity yesterday you need to eat."

Mitch sat down across from her. She looked at his crooked smile and bedroom eyes. The scar on his chin, and the laugh lines that bracketed his mouth only added to his appeal. She could get used to mornings like this.

Whoa, slow down. You're here for the free-range beef ad, not the sexy Wyoming cowboy.

"Did you want to continue our discussion from yesterday?" she asked.

Mitch checked his watch. "Can't now, I'm due down at the breeding pen. Kid Knight is scheduled to cover Dancer's Lady. I need to be there."

Rebecca tried to hide her disappointment that she wasn't able to go with him, recalling the years on her pop's horse farm. "Then you go. I'll clean up here and get some work done."

She carried her plate to the sink, thinking she should call Brent and run some ideas by him. She could use this quiet time to her advantage.

Mitch came up beside her. "I don't have a problem if you'd like to go with me."

She stared at him. "You won't mind?"

His eyes met hers. "You know how to handle yourself around horses."

"I would like to see your breeding operation," she told him.

Mitch tossed the towel on the counter. "Then let's go."

Together they left the house, and strolled to the

barn. Rebecca was determined to forget about work and enjoy this time. Yesterday she'd realized how much she missed being around horses. Maybe when she returned to New York she could find a stable and do a bit of riding on the weekends. It would be good to have something else in her life.

Mitch escorted Rebecca into the cool barn where six mares were housed in spacious stalls. The wooden gates were painted cream with hunter-green trim, as was the outside of the structure.

All dozen stalls, the tack room and feeding bins were immaculate, just as she expected them to be. It was obvious the mares boarded received the best of care. No doubt their owners paid top dollar to be covered by one of the Tucker studs.

"This is impressive."

"I'm pretty proud of the operation myself. It's a lot of work, but I'm sure you know that."

A high-pitched whinny drew their attention. "I think Kid is getting anxious."

"Yeah, he knows there's a pretty filly waiting for him."

Mitch directed Rebecca along the aisle until they reached the corral where the beautiful stallion was prancing around a holding pen. No doubt he'd caught the scent of the mare. A warm breeze blew strands of Rebecca's hair against her face. Mitch reached out and brushed them back, his finger caressing her cheek.

"Will you be okay waiting here?"

She nodded. "Go on, before Kid breaks down the pen."

Just then Wally walked up. He tipped his hat. "Morning, Rebecca. I see Mitch brought you to see the operations."

"He was nice enough to let me look around." There was another whinny from Kid. "I promise to stay out of everyone's way."

Mitch glanced at his foreman. "Is Jake here?"

Wally nodded. "He's with his mare in the corral."

Suddenly Mitch wondered what he'd been thinking to bring Rebecca here. She was a distraction just being close by. Hell, she could be at the house and still bother him.

"Let's get going, then," Mitch said. He and Wally approached the corral. The mare's hind legs were hobbled and her tail wrapped. Lady was young and he couldn't risk his stud getting kicked. He shook hands with Jake, and went to get Kid.

Mitch needed to concentrate on handling his young stallion. Although he wanted nature to just take its course, he needed to lend a strong hand. Neither owner wanted any harm to come to their animals. While two ranch hands held the mare, he and Wally helped make the mounting go smoothly.

Once the act was successfully completed, Wally took charge of Kid and led him from the corral. Dancer's Lady was escorted back to her stall. There she would reside a few weeks to verify she'd been impregnated before returning to her owner's ranch.

Mitch removed his gloves and shook hands with Jake before he walked off to join Rebecca standing at the fence. His heart tightened at the sight of her. It had been a long time since he'd had a woman waiting for him.

"So what do you think of Kid?" he asked, trying to ignore the feelings she aroused in him.

"He's a magnificent animal," she said excitedly. "I hope you have him on your website."

Mitch couldn't hide his pride or his grin. "Of course. I'll show it to you later." He led her back toward the barn. "For now, I think we should take advantage of Greta and Colby being gone. I love them to death, but sometimes it's nice to be by myself, or with another adult."

"I don't mind the children," she admitted. "But what about the ad? Shouldn't we use this time to work on it?"

That was the last thing on his mind. "Is that all you think about?"

"It is, when I'm getting paid to do a job."

"Well, since I'm the one paying you, I say we take the morning off. Besides, you'll need to see the operation. Instead of by horseback, we'll take the truck. Come on, Rebecca. I know you want to."

She raised an eyebrow. "Do you think it's a good idea?"

Mitch wasn't going to think about what was good or bad. He didn't want to think at all. He just wanted to spend a few hours alone with this beautiful woman.

It was as simple as that…and as complicated as that.

Twenty minutes later, the beat-up Jeep bounced over the uneven ground, jarring Mitch and Rebecca in their seats. Mitch glanced toward the passenger seat. Rebecca had a tight grip on the safety handle as she looked around.

He downshifted and steered the Jeep into the steep climb up the hillside. Finally he reached the top and parked along the ridge. Turning off the engine, he leaned back in his seat and looked out at the view.

"Well, what do you think?" he asked her, finding he wanted to impress her.

She was silent for what seemed like a long time. "It's amazing. The view is incredible."

"Glad you like it." Mitch looked in one direction where the ranch compound was neatly laid out below them. In another direction rose the powerful Rocky Mountains range where pine trees dotted the landscape and the green valley below much like a plush carpet.

"Look, Mitch," she called, pointing out her open window. "There's your herd."

He leaned toward her and caught a whiff of her hair, reminding him of wild flowers. He pulled back from the temptation.

"That's Freedom Valley, all right," he told her. "Since it's been free of all chemical fertilizers we thought that name seemed to suit it."

Rebecca smiled. "I like it."

"I have to confess, it was Greta's idea."

"She's a clever girl."

He didn't want to talk about his kids. "So, do you like my backyard?"

Once again Rebecca took in the panoramic view. "Let's see, the Rocky Mountains, lush green valleys and an endless blue sky." She sighed. "It's incredible! How do you ever get any work done?"

"That's the best part. I get to be outside all the time. There's a downside, too. It's pretty cold in the winter. In fact we usually get snowed in at least once a year."

"Sounds like fun to me," she said. "Of course, you have to have heat and food."

"We try to stay prepared." He definitely hadn't been prepared for Rebecca Valentine coming into his life. "We have generators, and if those fail we all just hover around the fireplace." He sighed remembering the last time. Carrie had just discovered she was pregnant. He'd been so worried about her delicate condition, but Carrie had only wanted to make love in the firelight. Then suddenly his idyllic life had ended when another snowstorm had taken his wife and unborn child from him.

Rebecca leaned back against the seat drawing his attention. "That reminds me of Poppy's and Nana's farm. Virginia isn't nearly as cold as Wyoming, but storms can take out the power." She closed her eyes. "We had fun sleeping in front of the fire."

Suddenly the picture of Rebecca snowed in with him formed in his head. Both of them wrapped up in blankets in front of a fire, using their body heat to keep warm. Damn. That was a daydream to stir a man's blood.

Mitch shook away the thought. "Are your grandparents still in Virginia?"

"No, they sold the farm years ago, and both passed away a few years back. Nana died after complications from a stroke, and Poppy soon followed. I don't think he could handle being alone." Her voice grew soft. "They were the most loving couple I ever knew." She turned to Mitch. "What about your parents?"

"Oh, yeah, they're alive and well, thank goodness. They've been living in Florida for the past six years. Mom couldn't take the cold weather any more. Years before Dad turned the ranch operation over to me. So there wasn't any reason for them not to spend the winters in the sunshine state. Lately, they've just stayed all year round." He sighed. "They wanted to move back here when Carrie died to help with the kids, but I told them I needed to do it on my own."

"That was nice of them."

Rebecca smiled at him, reminding him again that he was alone in a car with a beautiful woman. It had been a long time since he'd had such strong feelings for the opposite sex. He hadn't seen it coming, and he wasn't sure it was a good thing. He just knew he liked the feeling.

"You're doing a good job with Greta and Colby."

"Thanks. Being an only child, I always wanted a houseful." Mitch blinked. "Speaking of kids, I nearly forgot." He checked his watch. "Jimmy will be back with mine soon."

"Then you should be there," Rebecca said. "You must know how much Greta worries about you."

"I know. She's becoming quite the mother hen." He started the Jeep. "There's a short cut back, but it's pretty rough terrain."

She raised an eyebrow. "You think I can't handle it?"

He caught her mischievous look. No doubt she could, but he was more concerned about himself. Was he going to survive Rebecca Valentine?

"Buckle your seat belt, darlin'," he told her as he started up the Jeep. "Let's see what you New Yorkers are made of."

* * *

The following afternoon, Mitch sat behind his desk in the den. The last thing he wanted to do was spend the afternoon inside. But he'd promised Rebecca they'd go over some ideas.

He'd rather have a repeat of yesterday. Take a lazy ride around the ranch in a Jeep with a pretty woman, a woman who was genuinely interested in the ranch operation. He smiled to himself. Remembering the roller-coaster ride home, he wondered how she had ended up in New York City when she seemed to love open spaces.

Suddenly Colby scurried into the room followed by his sister. "I get to come to the meeting, too, don't I, Dad?" the boy asked as he went to the oak desk where Mitch sat.

Mitch came out of his reverie. "Of course you do, son. But remember what I said. You have to sit still and only talk when it's your turn."

"Dad!" Greta gave an exaggerated sigh. "You know he's just going to cause trouble."

"You both sit down and stop arguing." He directed them to the chairs beside the desk. "Greta, I know you've spent a lot of time on this project, and I appreciate all your work, but I'm going to run the meeting." Whoever thought he'd have to say that to his eleven-year-old daughter? What had happened to his baby girl?

When Greta opened her mouth, he raised his hand.

"Although we are partners, I'm still the parent here," he said. Why didn't he sound convincing? "Now, you can sit in on this meeting, and are allowed to give me your opinion, but in the end I make the final decisions."

Colby was already losing interest, but Greta just looked more determined. "Do you agree?" he asked.

"Sure, Dad," Colby told him, pulling his favorite Hot Wheels car from his jeans pocket, the red one with the white racing stripe. Greta took out a small tablet, ready to take notes.

There was a soft knock and he glanced up to see Rebecca standing in the doorway.

He stood. "Rebecca, please come in."

"Thank you," she said.

She was dressed in dark pleated slacks and a white blouse and with her hair pulled back into a bun. She was definitely back in business mode. He recalled her yesterday with her hair blowing free as they rode over the hillside. She was smiling and laughing as the Jeep bounced her up and down in her seat. Never once had she complained. He preferred that woman.

"Hi, Greta and Colby," she said as she placed her slim portfolio on the desk. "Is everyone ready?" she asked.

"Sure." He pulled over a chair to the group. "Please, sit down."

As she took the chair he offered he caught another

whiff of her soft scent. He moved behind the desk, out of the line of fire. He needed a clear head for business.

Rebecca drew a breath to ease her tension. She'd been trying to get an official meeting together since she'd arrived here three days ago. Now that it was happening, she found she was nervous.

"First, let me say I enjoyed riding out to see some of the ranch and the free-range herd. I also hope I can come up with an ad campaign that you all like."

"Are you going to take pictures of our steers?" Colby asked.

"If we decide that's what we want to do," Mitch said. "Son, please don't interrupt."

"I don't mind questions," Rebecca said as she turned to Mitch. "If it's okay with you?"

Mitch nodded.

"Although I've done extensive research on free-range beef, this is my first time on a cattle ranch. I'll need your help with where we should direct our marketing."

"The Internet," Greta said.

"That was my thought, too," Rebecca agreed. "I found several websites for free-range beef that you can order right online. We'll also have to direct our focus to soliciting food stores and fine restaurants." She opened her folder and started thumbing through her notes, realizing her hand was trembling. Why was she so nervous? She did presentations all the time. She stole a glance at Mitch and found him watching her. "I worked on the ideas we started on yesterday." She began to read when Colby raised his hand.

Mitch turned toward to the boy. "What is it, son?"

"Dad has a website for his stallions, Kid Knight and Stormy Knight," Colby volunteered. "He has their pictures and pictures of their foals. They're all over the world."

Rebecca felt herself blush as she recalled Kid Knight in action yesterday. "Then maybe we should do the same thing for the beef."

"Wow, are we going to sell our beef all over the world, too?"

She smiled at the child. "Maybe we'll start closer to home, Colby. There's a large market in cities like New York and San Francisco. There are restaurants that specialize in free-range beef. Of course, your herd is still young," she said and glanced at Mitch. "When will the first steers be ready to market?"

"Next week we're rounding them up and moving them into the feed lot. It'll be early winter before they go to slaughter."

"That gives us time to get together a target client list. Mitch, I'm sure you realize how much your business connections are going to help with the promotion of your product. And people will recognize the Tucker name. That list of contacts will help us."

"I'll see what I can come up with," he told her as he wrote something down.

"Good." Rebecca opened her folder and pulled out a rough mock-up of an ad. All three of the Tuckers leaned forward to have a closer look.

"Since you've decided to use the family name, I came up with some more ideas that I wanted to run by you." She pointed to the bold print. "'Tucker, a name you've trusted for years. Three generations of Tucker beef. Tucker's Best Beef.' And a slogan maybe something like: 'We'll stake our family's name on an unrivaled quality product.'"

There were empty spots for pictures of the family and ranch. "Greta's suggestion to use the Tucker name is a good one. It will be a great ad for the website. You will need to hire a promotion staff to make contact with buyers for specialty stores and restaurants." She waved her hand. "But that's down the line. We need to lay the groundwork now."

"Tucker's Best Beef," Mitch repeated. "Not bad."

"I think it's cool, too, Dad," Colby said. "Can I go play?"

"Sure, son." Colby took off and Mitch looked at his daughter. "How do you like it, Greta?"

"I like it a lot," she said, her blue eyes wide. "Maybe we can use Blackie in some pictures for the website."

Mitch groaned. His clever daughter had managed to work the calf in. But he had to admit it wasn't a bad idea. "I knew you were going to make a pet out of that steer."

She stood next to Rebecca. "Daddy, if Blackie is in the pictures, we have to keep him around. He's like our trademark."

Mitch looked at Rebecca and tried to act stern. "Did you two cook this up?"

Rebecca caught on to Mitch's teasing. She admired the way he connected with his children. "No, but I like how Greta thinks." She slipped her arm around his daughter. "We girls have to stick together."

"Dad, we should vote on making Blackie our mascot."

"Ranchers don't have steers as mascots," he said, but his expression softened. "Okay, I'll think about it." He stood. "I better go get Colby. It's our turn to cook. I'm a little tired of casseroles, so I thought I would grill some steaks for supper. Unless you ladies have a problem with that."

Greta raised an eyebrow. "As long as it isn't Blackie."

Mitch threw up his hands in mock defeat. "Blackie's safe for now. But when he outgrows that cute stage, he's history." He walked out.

The father/daughter banter made Rebecca smile. Mitch Tucker was handsome, sexy, a nice guy and a great father. It was the latter that drew her to him the most. And it was the best reason for her to stay away.

* * *

That evening, Mitch stood at the large stainless steel grill on the backyard deck, enjoying the peacefulness of dusk. He checked the steaks, making sure that they weren't overcooked. An easy task unless your mind was on something or someone else.

Rebecca Valentine.

She'd distracted him since the day she'd arrived. And as the days passed it seemed to be getting worse. His thoughts turned to Carrie.

From the moment he'd met her in college, Caroline Colby had been the love of his life. After they'd married Carrie had been more than willing to help him when he'd taken over the family business from his father. They'd had a good life and she'd traveled with him until Greta. Both being only children, they'd wanted a large family, but it had taken a while for her to conceive Colby. His business obligations might have had a lot to do with it because he'd had to travel a lot and that had cut into their time together. He'd tried to slow down, but he'd needed to travel to be successful.

Mitch turned the steaks.

For the rest of his life, he'd feel guilty that he hadn't been home when Carrie had been involved in an automobile accident. He'd only arrived at the hospital just in time to tell her how much he loved her.

Carrie had known she wasn't going to make it.

They'd cried together, but she'd made him promise to go on with his life, to take time and enjoy the kids, and not to mourn her long, but to find someone else to love. He'd thought she was crazy at the time. He'd never be able to replace her; he'd never be able to want another woman. But it had been a lonely two years and too many in front of him to live alone. And there was that longing to have more kids.

Mitch looked heavenward. What would Carrie think of Rebecca? He heard his son calling him and glanced at the door.

"Hey, Dad, how much longer? I'm hungry."

Mitch smiled. "You can't rush the chef. Should be about five minutes."

That seemed to appease the boy, but Colby didn't go inside. Instead he sat down in a lawn chair. "Hey, Dad. Do you think Rebecca's pretty?"

He was caught off guard by the question. "Sure, she's a pretty lady."

"Do you think she's as pretty as Mom?"

"I thought your mother was the prettiest girl in Wyoming. But you've seen pictures of her. What do you think?"

Colby shrugged. "It's different in a picture." Those dark eyes bore into Mitch's. "I can't remember what Mom looked like." The boy's voice cracked.

Mitch's chest tightened as he knelt down in front

of his son. "I know. You were so young." He took Colby's hand. "You have to know that she loved you and Greta a lot."

He nodded. "I know." Colby remained silent for a long time, then asked, "Is it okay if I like Rebecca?"

He'd expected this. His son had always gravitated toward females. No doubt it was their soft voices and touch, and their instinctive nurturing ways. And he'd witnessed the special attention that Rebecca had given his son and daughter.

"Yes, it's okay to like Rebecca," he said. "It's hard not to. But, son, she's going back to New York in a few weeks."

"I know, but I want her to be my friend anyway." His eyes brightened. "Maybe she can come back for a visit."

Mitch knew it was unlikely the career woman would return, but found he wanted the same thing. "Maybe."

In bed, Rebecca rolled onto her side and pulled her legs up hoping to ease the cramps. Nothing had worked, not even the strong pain medicine the doctor had given her. She glanced at the clock. It was after midnight.

She sighed and finally got up, thinking some hot tea might help. Since all the Tuckers were in bed she wouldn't be disturbing anyone. She grabbed her robe and headed down the hall. Once she reached the kitchen she saw the light over the stove and the tea kettle. That was when she noticed the shadow by the window.

The figure was tall with wide shoulders. "Mitch," she whispered.

"Rebecca. What are you doing up?"

He stepped into the light and she saw he was only wearing a pair of jeans. She couldn't help but stare at his bare, well-developed chest and those muscular arms and shoulders. "I…thought I'd get a cup of tea, but I don't want to disturb you." She turned to leave when he took her by the arm.

"Rebecca, you don't have to leave. I guess we both had the same problem. I couldn't sleep, either."

Suddenly her stomach clenched and she nearly doubled over.

"Rebecca, what's wrong?"

She tried to wave him off. "It's just cramps."

"It doesn't look to be just cramps." He took her by her arm and led her into the family room. "Here, lie down."

"Mitch, you don't need to worry about this. Hot tea should help."

He sat her down on the sofa. "I know I'm just an insensitive male, but I was married for a dozen years. I know a few remedies that might help. I'll be right back."

He left and, in too much discomfort to argue,

Rebecca stretched out on the cushion. Soon Mitch returned with a heating pad and placed it on her stomach and plugged it in, then left her again. This time he came back with two steaming cups of tea.

"I hope you like Earl Grey?"

"I'm half English. I'll drink any kind of tea."

Mitch sat on the edge of the coffee-table, close to her. Too close. She pushed herself up but her feet were still curled under her. He watched her sip from her cup, and drank his own.

"How's the heating pad doing?"

She patted her stomach. "It's helping. Thank you."

With more tea she felt herself relaxing until she caught Mitch staring at her.

Placing the cup on the table, Rebecca smoothed her hair back as best she could. "I know I look a mess."

To Mitch, the moonlight shining through the window only emphasized her beauty. "You look fine. Besides, just worry about your…condition." He reached for the blanket off the back of the sofa and covered her. "Just rest and let the heat relax your muscles." Instead of resuming his seat on the table, he moved to the edge of the cushions. He knew he was too close, but he couldn't seem to back away. Their eyes connected, and his throat went dry. She had to feel the heat between them.

"I feel better," she breathed. "Thank you."

"No problem." Oh, but there was a big problem. The way she made him feel whenever he got close. The way she kept him awake at night, dreaming about what it would be like to touch her…to kiss her…

"I think my medicine is kicking in."

Something was kicking in with him, too. "Good. And tomorrow morning, I want you to sleep in."

"Oh, there's no need for that."

"Just take the morning for yourself. In the afternoon, we'll all drive out to the feed lot, and, if there's time, to the construction site for the meat-packing plant."

"I'd like that," she said with a bright smile. "Have I told you how much fun I'm having doing this job?"

He was excited by her obvious pleasure. "I think you're enjoying being out of the rat race."

"Could be," she admitted. "The quiet here is soothing. And being with Colby and Greta has been nice."

"What about me?" he asked. "Do I live up to my reputation as a tyrant?"

She gasped. "I never heard that…"

He began to laugh. "I'm not the easiest man to work with."

"I haven't found that," she admitted. "You've been fair and open to new ideas, and you're not a bad cook."

"You haven't been hard to take, either, Rebecca

Valentine." He leaned closer. He could feel the side of her hip against his. "I thought for sure that a gung-ho woman would arrive who wouldn't want to step foot out of the house, let alone ride a horse. Little did I know that you grew up on a farm." His voice lowered. "To say the least, you were quite a surprise."

"I was?"

He couldn't help it. He touched her cheek. Her skin was as soft as he imagined. "A beautiful surprise," he repeated. His head lowered and his mouth caressed hers gently.

Rebecca sucked in a breath, but that didn't stop him. He went back and took more. He burrowed his fingers in her wild hair. When she didn't resist, he settled his mouth on hers, parting her lips in the process. He groaned and his arms wrapped around her, pulling her close.

A surge of need seared his body like a hot poker. When her fingers locked behind his neck and clung to him, he almost lost it. His pulse was pounding in his ears as he savored the taste and feel of her. Finally the air was gone from his lungs and he broke off the kiss.

They were both breathing hard. Oh, Lord, he wanted…nothing more than to carry her upstairs to his bed. But, somehow, common sense prevailed and he released her.

"I'm not going to apologize for the kiss, but it would be best if I say goodnight." He got up and walked away.

It was the last thing he wanted to do.

CHAPTER FIVE

SHE was a coward.

Rebecca paced her bedroom trying to get up the courage to face Mitch. How was she supposed to act after her client had kissed the living daylights out of her last night, and, worse, she'd kissed him right back? Her stomach tightened at the thought of being in Mitch's arms, having his mouth on hers.

"Stop it," she ordered herself as she shook away the memory. This wasn't helping the problem. How should she act when they'd both gone over the line?

Well, first thing was not to make too much out of it. Right. Her career was everything to her, and she wasn't going to mess that up. Besides, she was returning to New York so there was no future for them.

She glanced at the bedside clock. It was nearly eight o'clock. Maybe her immediate problem wasn't so immediate. He'd probably already gone down to the barn to start his day.

"Well, for sure I can't stay in my room all day."

Squaring her shoulders, Rebecca opened the door and headed down the hall. "He kissed me. So what?" she murmured. "If anyone should be embarrassed, it should be him."

With renewed courage, Rebecca walked into the kitchen but was disappointed to find the room empty except for Greta.

The girl got up from the table. "Good, you're awake. Dad said to let you sleep because you weren't feeling well last night. Are you better today?"

"Much better," Rebecca told her, realizing she did feel pretty good. "Where is everyone?"

"Dad and Colby are down at the barn waiting for the bus."

"What bus?"

Greta smiled. "First eat breakfast, and I'll take you down so Dad can tell you." The girl went to the stove and brought back a plate of food and put it on the table.

Rebecca needed coffee. She turned to the coffee-maker, poured a cup and took a drink. "Help do what?"

"It's a surprise, but it'll be fun. So eat."

Rebecca glanced down at the heaped plate of bacon and eggs. "Your dad needs to stop feeding me like this."

"Dad always cooks too much." Greta giggled. "Just eat half of it and we'll go."

The girl's excitement was contagious. "Give me a hint."

"Well, let's just say it has to do with kids. You like kids, don't you?"

"I'm crazy about kids." That was her problem.

Mitch kept looking toward the house, for a sign of Greta. Maybe Rebecca still wasn't feeling good, or she'd decided she didn't want to come down. Maybe she regretted last night. No. Not the way she'd kissed him back.

Maybe he'd had no business kissing her. Except for the fact that he hadn't been able to resist any longer, and, if she was as willing as last night, he planned on kissing her again.

"Dad, the bus is coming," Colby yelled from his perch on top of the corral fence.

"Okay, son," Mitch said as he turned toward the row of his gentlest horses, saddled and ready for their young riders. Nearby were a half-dozen ranch hands who had volunteered for this task.

"Dad, we're here," Greta called as she and Rebecca hurried toward him.

Mitch's focus was on Rebecca. His heart did a funny skip as he saw how natural she looked in jeans and boots, and how her beautiful hair was down, held away from her face by silver clips.

"Hi," he managed, wondering if she had lain

awake half the night remembering what had happened between them.

"Hi." She placed a straw cowboy hat on her head.

"How do you feel this morning?" he asked.

"Much better, thank you." She glanced at the horses. "What's going on? Greta was very mysterious."

Mitch smiled. "In about two minutes there'll be a dozen kids here, eager to ride. I was hoping I could count on you to help out."

She blinked those big blue-gray eyes at him. "Sure, but I'm not qualified to teach—"

"There's no teaching involved, Rebecca. These kids just want to ride a horse around the arena. They're kids with special needs. So basically you'll help us get them in the saddle and lead the horse around the corral. You can handle a horse."

She nodded. "Of course. Whatever you need me to do."

Mitch could see she was distant and he had to find out why. "Rebecca, can I have a quick word with you?" Before she could answer him, he led her away from the kids. "About last night…and what happened between us… I never want you to feel uncomfortable around me. If I took advantage of the situation…"

"Mitch, we both were responsible for what happened. I want you to understand that I'm usually more professional than that; I haven't let my personal feelings get in the way of business."

"I never thought you did. Rebecca, you did nothing wrong, and neither did I."

"We overstepped, Mitch. I'm here to work—"

He'd opened his mouth to argue when the bus's horn sounded. He looked up to see the small yellow school bus coming down the road, kicking up dust in its wake.

"We'll talk about this later," he told her, not giving her a chance to protest. "But just one thing, Rebecca: I'm not sorry I kissed you. And I think you enjoyed it as much as I did." As a matter of fact, he wanted to kiss that shocked look off her face, right now, but he hadn't the time to do it justice. "Now, we've got to help the kids.

She followed him. "Mitch, wait. You can't say that and walk off." Her voice lowered. "Whether we enjoyed it or not isn't the question. It can't happen again."

"We'll talk about it later," he said.

Rebecca was fuming, but she followed Mitch. He welcomed the teachers as they came off the bus, then turned to help the excited kids down the steps.

"Hi, Mitch," several of the children called in greeting as they lined up.

He went to them and gave high fives and hugs all around. "Hey, kids, I want you to meet a friend of mine. Her name is Rebecca and she grew up on a horse farm. She's going to help you ride today."

"Hi, Rebecca," they choroused.

"Hi," she said, then Mitch introduced her to two teachers, Kathy Sanders and Peggy Anderson.

Rebecca was assigned to a beautiful five-year-old boy named Matthew. The boy didn't speak to her, but his blue eyes told her of his excitement. She took his hand and together they walked to the spotted mare.

"Magic," Matthew said.

A ranch hand, Neil, was holding the horse's reins. "That's right, Matthew, you're riding Magic today." He handed a helmet to Rebecca. "He needs to wear this."

She secured it under his chin. "Okay, Matthew. Let's get this strapped on." The child stood patiently until she finished. Neil lifted the boy into the saddle and strapped him in with a safety harness. Rebecca stepped back, until the task was completed, focused on the big grin on the five-year-old's face.

Neil handed her the reins. "You take the lead, I'll spot him." At her nod, he moved to the side of the horse's rump.

"You ready for a ride, Matthew?" she asked.

"Ride…" Matthew said. "Go…Magic."

Rebecca smiled as she tugged on the reins and joined the circle of horses walking around the corral. She stayed close to the boy, making sure he was holding on, then watched the other leaders and riders.

In the front of the group was Wally, walking Colby's horse, Trudy, with a little girl perched in the saddle. One of the teachers was at the rider's side, and behind them came Greta and Jimmy. Greta led the horse, but her eyes were on the young ranch hand. It was obvious that the girl had a crush on the handsome teenage boy.

Rebecca's attention turned to the next rider, Mitch's charge, an older boy of about eight, whom Mitch had charge of. He was showing the child how to do commands for his horse. Then he walked the horse to the center of the arena, where several colorful stuffed animals sat on top of the closed barrel.

"What's the command, Tim?" Mitch asked.

"Stop, Rudy," the boy called out. The horse stopped next to the barrel.

"Red, Tim."

The boy paused a moment, then reached down and picked up the red squirrel.

"Good job, Tim," Mitch said.

The boy's face beamed, his pleasure obvious as Mitch walked the horse to the other barrel.

Rebecca glanced up at Matthew to see he was watching the activity. "Matthew, do you want to do that?"

The boy pointed. "Monkey."

"Well, let's go get the monkey." With Neil's help

Matthew retrieved the stuffed animal. The next hour passed quickly, but it wasn't until the kids headed for the bus that she realized her fatigue.

She helped Matthew onto the bus. He looked at her and said, "Bye, Becca."

Her heart melted, and tears pricked her eyes. "Bye, Matthew." She waved and stepped back as the teachers strapped the children in their safety seats, and the bus drove off.

She felt Mitch's presence as he came up behind her. "They tug at your heart," he said.

"How long have you been doing this?"

"A few years, but only from May through October," he said as leaned back against the fence. "With the weather and round-ups, there isn't more time."

"I'd say it's pretty incredible for you to open your ranch for the time you have."

He smiled. "It's easy. I'm crazy about kids, but I can't take credit for the project. Carrie started it about three years ago. Her cousin's boy is autistic, and when she saw how much he responded to horses at her parents' ranch in Cheyenne, she decided to help other kids with special needs locally. It was Carrie's dream to have a summer camp here."

They both were silent, watching the ranch hands lead the horses back to their stalls. Colby and Greta hurried after Wally into the barn.

"What a great idea," Rebecca finally said. "Maybe we can work the plans so some profit from the beef can go to support the camp."

Mitch's gaze locked with hers. As much as she tried to glance away, he wouldn't allow it. "Rebecca... you're the first woman I've kissed since Carrie died."

She tried to act unaffected, but it didn't work.

"It's not that there weren't opportunities," he went on. "I just haven't wanted to. Until last night. Until you."

"It still shouldn't have happened, Mitch." She felt the tremble in her voice. "I'm here on business—"

"Can you just forget about business for a minute? We kissed, Rebecca, and I want to kiss you again. I also know that we have to work together."

"And I'll be returning to New York soon."

His mouth twitched. "Not that soon."

Rebecca's heart was pounding hard. It would be so easy just to let this happen, but she couldn't. In the end, she would only get hurt. She couldn't dream about a husband and a family. It was too late for that.

"I have a job to do, Mitch. My career is important to me."

He grew serious as he pushed away from the wall and stepped in front of her. "Take it from me, Rebecca—don't let it be everything. You need to have something else in your life." He released a long breath. "Fame and fortune don't mean anything unless you have someone to share it with." A smile appeared across that handsome face of his. "Be warned, Rebecca Valentine, as long as you're here, I'm going to try and convince you of that."

As hard as she tried, Rebecca couldn't put Mitch's words out of her head. She decided she would spend less time with the Tucker family. Then, Mitch announced that no one was cooking tonight—he was taking them all into town for supper.

Rebecca tried to beg off, but when Colby asked her to "Please, come," she couldn't turn him down. The kids climbed in the back of the Range Rover and Mitch held the door so she could get in the passenger seat. This time she wore dress slacks so she didn't have to worry about exposing too much leg.

"I've decided pants are more practical for SUVs."

Mitch's eyes gleamed as he leaned closer. "I'm a little disappointed," he whispered in her ear. "You've got great legs."

The huskiness of his voice sent a shiver down her spine. Before she could say anything he walked around to the driver's side and took his seat. The thirty-minute ride into town focused on the kids, the movies they wanted to see and other activities. Rebecca enjoyed listening to the easy banter between parent and children.

It wasn't long before they pulled into the parking lot of the local family-style restaurant, The Country Kitchen. Inside was cozy, with café-style curtains in the windows and checked table-cloths on the tables. Colby hurried to one of the red-vinyl booths beside the large window. Greta slid in next to him, leaving Rebecca and Mitch to sit side by side.

A slim waitress of about forty walked over. She was dressed in a starched white blouse and dark slacks. Her color-treated blonde hair was pulled into a French twist and her name tag read "Wanda". She set down four glasses of water and smiled.

"Well, if it isn't the Tucker family. What brings ya'll into town? A special occasion?"

"Hi, Wanda," Greta said.

"Hi, Wanda," Colby echoed. "Dad's treating us 'cause we're tired of cooking."

Dancing hazel eyes turned to Mitch. "So you ran out of Margie's casseroles."

"No," Mitch said. "We just decided to come into town and show Rebecca around."

"Well, it ought to take about fifteen minutes," she teased and held out her hand to Rebecca. "Hi, I'm Wanda Shaw. I went to school with Mitchell here, but it seems he forgot his manners about introductions." She sighed. "I guess I'm gonna have to tattle to his mother in Florida."

Rebecca got a kick out of seeing Mitch blush. "I'm Rebecca Valentine. I'm here to help market the Tuckers' free-range beef project."

"As if Wanda doesn't know all about what goes on in this town," Mitch accused. "I'm sure Greta and Colby told her all she wants to know."

Wanda straightened. "Well, people expect to come in here and know what's going on."

"Since you know everything already, you can bring us each a Calvin's burger with all the trimmings." He looked at Rebecca. "Is that okay with you?"

She nodded. "And I'll have a diet cola to drink."

"Dad, can we have soda, too?" Greta pleaded.

He looked thoughtful, then nodded.

They cheered and Colby said, "I want orange soda, please."

"And lemon-lime soda for me, please," Greta said.

Mitch turned to Rebecca. "You could have ordered something besides a hamburger. Cal has great specials."

She inhaled the scent of his aftershave. He was too close. "No, I like hamburgers."

"They're my favorite." Colby frowned. "But I hate onions. Greta doesn't like them either 'cause it makes her breath stink and she can't kiss boys."

Greta gasped. "That's a lie."

"No, it's not," Colby argued. "That's what you told Sarah Peterson."

A blush spread across Greta's cheeks. "You were listening at my door. Dad!"

Mitch raised a hand. "We're not going to discuss this now, but Colby, what you did was wrong. I'll be talking to you at home."

The boy hung his head. "Okay, I'm sorry, Greta. I won't do it again."

"You better not," his sister fumed.

"I don't know why anyone would want to kiss a girl anyway," the boy muttered. "It's dumb. I'm never gonna do that."

Rebecca could barely contain her laughter. Then Mitch turned toward her, but he wasn't smiling.

"When you get older, son, you'll think differently." His gaze held hers for a long time, then finally he turned away and looked at his daughter. "Since when are you kissing boys?"

"Dad…I'm not…" Greta's wide-eyed gaze sought Rebecca for help.

Rebecca reached for Mitch's hand to stop the interrogation. "I remember when I was Greta's age, my sister and I used to talk about boys all the time. But that's all it was, just talk." Surprisingly, Rebecca felt Mitch's hand grasp hers. "That's what girls do. We dream, we fantasize…"

"I was only thinking about fast cars and horses at Greta's age," Mitch told her.

NO POSTAGE
NECESSARY
IF MAILED
IN THE
UNITED STATES

BUSINESS REPLY MAIL

FIRST-CLASS MAIL   PERMIT NO. 717-003   BUFFALO, NY

POSTAGE WILL BE PAID BY ADDRESSEE

SILHOUETTE READER SERVICE
3010 WALDEN AVE
PO BOX 1867
BUFFALO NY 14240-9952

Get FREE BOOKS and a FREE GIFT when you play the...

LAS VEGAS
GAME

*Just scratch off
the gold box with a coin.
Then check below to see
the gifts you get!*

YES! I have scratched off the gold box. Please send me my **2 FREE BOOKS** and **gift for which I qualify.** I understand that I am under no obligation to purchase any books as explained on the back of this card.

310 SDL EFXZ   **210 SDL EFWQ**

FIRST NAME   LAST NAME

ADDRESS

APT.#   CITY

STATE/PROV.   ZIP/POSTAL CODE

(S-R-08/06)

7	7	7	Worth TWO FREE BOOKS plus a BONUS Mystery Gift!
🍒	🍒	🍒	Worth TWO FREE BOOKS!
🔔	🔔	♣	TRY AGAIN!

www.eHarlequin.com

Offer limited to one per household and not valid to current Silhouette Romance® subscribers. All orders subject to approval.

Rebecca laughed. "That's because boys don't mature as quickly as girls."

"Yeah, Dad," Greta said. "Maturity-wise, girls are ahead of boys." She giggled. "But at about twenty-one you guys finally catch up to us."

Mitch couldn't believe this was his daughter talking. Where did she get this stuff? "Twenty-one? How do you know this?"

The preteen rolled her eyes. "In Sex Ed."

Before Mitch could respond, Rebecca squeezed his fingers under the table and Wanda arrived with the drinks. Rebecca released his hand and he immediately hated the loss of contact, but wasn't going to let her keep pulling away for long.

Rebecca hadn't laughed so much in years. She truly liked being with the Tuckers. It had been a long time since she'd felt like a part of a family. Not since she and Rachel had spent summers with her grandparents.

She stole a glance at the man seated next to her. Mitch Tucker would be a hard man to forget, along with his kids. No matter how unwise, she couldn't seem to keep her distance from him.

Mitch tossed down money for the check and tip when someone called to him. He turned around and saw Mildred Evans, his mother's friend, coming toward him. Biting back a groan, he plastered a smile on his face as the older woman approached. He stood and greeted her.

"Mrs Evans, it's good to see you."

She smiled. "Good to see you, Mitchell." She looked down at the children. "Oh, my, you've all grown so much. This can't be Colby. Well, aren't you getting handsome? Just like your father." Her attention moved to his daughter. "And this is little Greta," she gushed. "Such a young lady, and the image of your beautiful mother."

"Thank you, Mrs Evans," Greta said.

"I'm only speaking the truth. We all miss Carrie so much." The older woman finally glanced Rebecca's way. "And who is this?"

"Mrs Evans, this is Rebecca Valentine. She's from the Pierce Agency and is helping with my free-range beef project. Rebecca, this is Mrs Evans. She's a friend of my parents."

"Nice to meet you, Mrs Evans," Rebecca said.

The woman gave Rebecca the once-over, and Mitch knew that his mother in Florida would get a full report in the morning.

"It's nice to meet you, Ms Valentine. I'm sure you feel like a fish out of water in our small town."

"It's a nice change of pace. And I've enjoyed staying at the Tucker ranch."

Mitch could see the older woman's mind clicking away. "It's so nice that Mitch opened his home to you."

He needed to end this, before the kids fed her any information. "Well, we should get going if we want to watch a movie before bedtime. It's been nice to see you, Mrs Evans."

Mitch quickly gathered the kids and Rebecca, and they were out the door and in the car without any further incident. All the way home, Rebecca was silent, probably because of what Mildred had said.

As promised, they watched a movie in the family room. Mitch wasn't sure which Disney movie it was, because he couldn't stop watching Rebecca. Ever since Mrs Evans' appearance tonight, she had pulled away from them, into what seemed like her own little world.

When the movie ended, Colby had fallen asleep. When Mitch scooped him up, his son protested and said he wanted Rebecca to go, too.

Rebecca agreed and followed the group upstairs. Mitch carried Colby to his room, stripped him down and put on his pajamas. Rebecca came in, but stood back.

She felt out of place. She'd never put a child to bed before. Not that she hadn't wanted to; she'd just never had the chance.

"Rebecca," a sleepy Colby called her, "I'm glad you went with us tonight. It was fun."

"I had fun, too."

Mitch finished dressing the child, and put him under the thin blanket.

"Dad, did you have fun with Rebecca?"

Mitch looked at Rebecca. "Yes, I did," he told his son and kissed his forehead. "Now, go to sleep, kiddo."

Rebecca came closer and couldn't resist brushing back the child's hair. "See you in the morning, Colby."

She followed Mitch out of his son's room. "If you don't mind, you better come with me for Greta."

She wanted nothing more, but this was the wrong direction if she was going to keep her distance. "Okay."

He tapped on the door. "Greta, you ready for bed?"

"Come in, Dad," she called.

Opening the door, he walked in. Rebecca decided to remain in the doorway.

The girl's room was all pink with a canopy bed and stuffed animals lining the top shelf of a bookcase. Greta sat on her bed, leaning against the headboard with a book. Her father went to her and leaned down to kiss her cheek.

"Don't stay up too late, honey."

"I won't, Dad," she said, then looked over at Rebecca. "Rebecca, I'm glad you went with us tonight. I had a good time."

"Yes, so did I," Rebecca said, even if she was getting too involved with her client's family.

"Maybe we can do it again." Greta glanced at her father. "Dad, why don't we go riding tomorrow?"

"As nice as that sounds, I have things to do. You know, I run a ranch."

"I thought Wally did."

"Someone has to tell him what to do. Besides, I have an appointment with a mare's owner. Goodnight, now, Greta."

"Goodnight, Greta. I'll see you in the morning. It's my turn to fix breakfast."

Mitch kissed his daughter, then walked out and closed the door. "You don't have to cook for my children," he said when Rebecca reached his side.

"And you don't have to wait on me, either," she said, trying to keep her voice down.

Mitch grabbed her hand and pulled her with him down the stairs, away from prying ears. "I told you, I'm fixing meals for myself and the kids so it would seem silly…" He paused. "Why are you suddenly acting like this?"

She glanced away. "I just feel that we've gotten off track a little…"

"So we took today off." He studied her for a moment with those incredible dark eyes. "But you're still thinking about the kiss."

"It shouldn't have happened," she said. "And maybe going out to dinner tonight wasn't wise either."

"You kissed me back, Rebecca." He moved in closer, forcing her back up against the banister. He placed his hands on either side of the railing. "You could have stopped me."

"I know," she whispered. "And I should have."

"Admit it, Rebecca, you didn't stop me because you wanted it as much as I did then, and we both do now." He slowly lowered his head to her. Try as she might, she couldn't seem to force out any words to deny it.

CHAPTER SIX

REBECCA shouldn't want this man, but she did. In fact she was starved for him. For his touch…his kiss, the feel of his body against hers.

"Come here, Becca," Mitch said in his husky voice. He reached for her and pulled her into his arms. She resisted for a moment, then relented, her arms sliding around his neck.

He tangled his hands in her hair, shifting so her body was flat against his. Then he closed his mouth over hers. A bolt of raw sensation knocked the wind right out of her lungs. But who needed to breathe?

Mitch shuddered as Rebecca moved against him. He was so close to the edge, it wouldn't take much to push him over. And she felt so good, smelled so good…tasted like heaven.

Unable to control his need, he widened his stance and eased her in closer. She whimpered and clutched at him. Mitch opened his mouth against hers, feeding on the hunger between them. Trying to regain some control, he buried his head against her neck. "You can't tell me that you don't want this," he whispered.

"That still doesn't mean it's right," she said breathlessly.

Mitch shifted against her. She couldn't help but feel what she did to him. "It feels pretty damn right to me." He captured her mouth once again and slipped his tongue inside to taste her. Hearing her whimper, he repeated the action. When he finally released her, his heart was pounding in his chest like a drum.

Rebecca grasped at the last of her common sense. She couldn't keep doing this. She was an emotional wreck, reacting to the moment, using Mitch for comfort. "We have to stop," she begged.

She moved out of his embrace. Unable to look at him she murmured goodnight and hurried off toward her bedroom. Once the door was closed, she walked to the bed and sank onto the mattress. She had no control when it came to Mitch Tucker.

And she had too many things to think about other than having an affair with him. Her hand covered her stomach, feeling the cramps that plagued her mid-section, reminding her that she couldn't have it all. It was just a shame she hadn't realized sooner that a family was the most important thing of all.

* * *

The next morning, Mitch was up early and out with Wally, who was getting ready to move the herd. It would take most of the day to get the steers into the feed lot and make sure they were settled for the next four months.

And he wanted to go along, but he couldn't leave the kids alone. So he got Jimmy's seventeen-year-old sister, Kelly, to come by for the day. He knew Greta would throw a fit, but he had no choice. This way, Rebecca could concentrate on getting some work done.

Rebecca. He'd thought about her all night. He shouldn't have pushed the situation with her. Whether or not she had feelings for him, it was clear she was struggling with her own demons and he was doing the same thing. He'd loved Carrie a long time. Now suddenly he had the hots for another woman, and it was quickly turning into more than that. And his kids were getting just as attached to Rebecca.

Was he ready for what came next?

Rebecca checked the clock again. It was after nine and Mitch hadn't returned to the house for breakfast. Not that she was anxious to see him, but she needed to talk to him. He needed to know her plans.

The back door opened and her heart began to race. She released a long breath as Mitch walked into the kitchen. He removed his hat and hung it on the hook. She couldn't help but stare at the good-looking man in the worn jeans and Western shirt. Who would have thought that she'd fall for a Wyoming cowboy?

She plastered on a smile. "Good morning."

"Good morning," he returned and went to the coffeepot. "Where are the kids?"

"I asked Greta to take Colby outside."

"I'm sorry. Were they bothering you?"

"No, they've never bothered me. This is about you and me. Last night…what happened between us wasn't wise."

He leaned against the counter and took a sip of coffee. "Because we're working together?"

"That's most of it. But being in your house, with your kids… I don't feel right about starting something."

He set down his mug and came to her. "Look, Rebecca, I'm so rusty at this. I've forgotten all the rules. I haven't even taken the time to date anyone." His dark eyes bored into hers. "But I do know I'm attracted to you, and I believe you're attracted to me. Isn't that a good beginning?"

"No! You're my client."

"And that's interfering with what?"

"Everything!"

"Is there someone else in your life?"

"No!"

He looked relieved. "Okay," he began. "I'll back off because we need to get this project going."

"And my returning to New York for a while will help."

He frowned. "You're leaving?"

"I want to get things set up with our art department. And I need to touch base with my other clients." She also had a doctor's appointment she couldn't cancel. "I should be back in a week or so."

Suddenly a loud scream drew their attention. Then the back door slammed, and Greta rushed in with Colby. His leg was cut and bleeding.

"What happened?" Mitch lifted his crying son and seated him on the counter. Rebecca went to the sink, grabbed a clean towel and ran water over it.

Greta's face was flushed. "He was climbing on the wood pile… I told him to get down, but he didn't listen to me." Tears streamed down her face. "He fell off and got caught on a nail."

Rebecca came over and handed Mitch the towel. "No, you do it," Colby begged her.

With her own heart pounding in panic, she saw the strained look of a worried father. "Go ahead, you can handle it." He handed her the cloth.

Rebecca tried to soothe the boy. "It's going to be okay, Colby. Just take a deep breath and blow it out."

The child did as she asked, and she began to clean

the big gash in his leg. She looked at Mitch and spoke softly. "I think he should see a doctor."

Mitch nodded. "Let's go." He scooped up his son.

Rebecca followed with Greta. In the car she sat in the back seat with Colby while Mitch phoned the doctor. When they reached the small emergency room, Dr Walters was already waiting for them.

Rebecca stayed with Greta in the reception area trying to concentrate on the TV and not what was happening to a little five-year-old boy.

Seeing that Greta was upset, Rebecca slipped an arm around her shoulders and said, "What happened to Colby was an accident."

"He never listens to me," Greta said. "I tell him things all the time and he just does what he wants."

"That's a little boy for you. The big boys are the same way."

They both laughed, then Greta quickly sobered. "Do you think he's hurt really bad?"

Rebecca shook her head. "The cut wasn't too deep, but he needed stitches. Colby will have a scar to brag about."

Great groaned. "I'm going to have to be his slave for ever."

"Well, he'd do the same for you."

The girl grew serious. "I know I act like I don't care about Colby much…but if something bad happened…"

Rebecca hugged her. "I know. You love him." She thought about her sister. All the years they hadn't spoken. Her heart ached. Maybe she should contact Rachel…

Mitch came out of the room, pushing a smiling Colby in a wheelchair.

"I got six stitches and a shot. And I didn't even cry." He cocked his head upward. "Huh, Dad?"

"No, you didn't." Mitch turned to Rebecca. He looked less stressed then he had when they'd brought Colby in. "He was a brave boy."

The boy grinned. "So how about we go get hamburgers?"

Greta looked at Rebecca. "See, he's already getting everything. Oh, I'm not going to be able to stand living with him."

Rebecca and Mitch exchanged a glance. She had an urge to hug him. But no. She was a visitor here. This wasn't her family.

The rest of the day, everyone catered to Colby's every wish. By the time the boy was put to bed they were all exhausted, including Greta, who had gone to her room.

Rebecca was in her bedroom when she decided she wanted a cup of tea. She wasn't the only one. In the dimly lit kitchen she found Mitch sitting in the dark, looking out the window. She started to leave, but when she heard his sob it tore at her heart.

She knew that desperate feeling of being totally alone. Against her better judgment she went to him.

"Mitch…"

He quickly wiped his eyes before he turned to her. "I thought everyone was in bed."

"I came for a cup of tea." She frowned. "We've all had a rough day and it took a lot out of us."

He nodded. The moonlight through the window showed his red eyes. "I felt so helpless today."

"You weren't, though. You called the doctor and got Colby to the hospital." She stepped closer to him, unable to keep from touching him. He needed someone. He needed her.

"Oh, Becca," he whispered, his head rested against her breasts. "I don't know what I would have done if something…"

"Shh… Don't borrow trouble, Mitch. Colby is all right."

"Damn, it's rough doing this alone." He stood and drew her close. "I wish you weren't leaving."

She weakened. "I guess I don't have to go right away. I can postpone my trip until Colby gets his stitches out."

He pulled back and looked down at her. "Are you sure?"

No, she wasn't sure of anything, any more. She nodded. "I'll need more time in your office."

"Tell you what, if you watch Colby in the mornings, I get Wally and the crew working for the day, and I'll take over for you in the afternoon. How does that work for you?"

"Just fine. But there's something else. We can't let this get any more personal."

"You mean no more kisses?"

She nodded.

He sighed. "You drive a hard bargain, lady. But if it's the only way to keep you here… So when does this new rule begin?" he asked as he drew her to him.

She was in big trouble. "Tomorrow," she breathed just as Mitch lowered his mouth to hers.

The next morning, Mitch hurried back to the house. He knew keeping his son in one spot for long was nearly impossible. Besides, he didn't mind seeing Rebecca.

His thoughts turned to the kiss they'd shared last night. There had been several last kisses. One had led to another and another, until he'd finally begged for mercy and given Rebecca a shove toward her bedroom.

The last thing he wanted to do was mess this up. He wanted Rebecca Valentine to stay so they could find out where these feelings were going. And he was going to do everything possible to find out, which might be the craziest thing he'd ever done. What if this didn't work out? No, something told him that Rebecca wanted more than her career.

He already knew she was great with his kids. She was a natural mother. Suddenly, he pictured Rebecca pregnant with his child. He stopped short trying to catch his breath. Had his feelings for her gone that far? He climbed on the porch, opened the back door and headed for the family room where he heard his son's favorite Power Ranger video playing. Colby sat on the sofa with his warrior figures in his hands.

Mitch glanced across the room. Rebecca sat at the table, looking over some papers. She had on jeans and a red polo shirt. Best of all, her glorious hair was hanging loose.

Colby finally spotted him. "Hey, Dad! What are you doing here?"

"I thought I'd check on you. I have a few minutes before going into town," he said, and went to ruffle his son's hair. He glanced at Rebecca. "Then I need to go with Wally to check on the herd. I might be a little late getting back."

"That's okay," Rebecca said.

"No, it's not, but I'll make sure that Greta is here to sit with Colby."

Rebecca smiled. "And I'll be close by if there's any trouble. But I doubt there will be. Your daughter is very mature for her age."

"You mean nearly twelve going on thirty." Mitch grew serious. "Sometimes I feel I stole her childhood from her. She suddenly had to grow up when Carrie died."

"It's hard losing a parent so young… At any age it's hard. Greta is an amazing young lady."

Mitch couldn't help but see a lot of the same traits in both females. "She really seems to relate to you," he said. "I feel I'm not going to be able to keep up with her."

"Just keep talking to her, make her feel special."

Mitch wondered if Rebecca's father's living in England made it difficult for them to have a relationship. "Every woman should be treated special. Was there someone who made you feel special when you were Greta's age?"

She glanced away. "In some families, when there's a divorce, the focus isn't on the children. But that's past history. You better get going. I'll let Greta know the arrangement." She stood and walked out of the room.

Rebecca wasn't real subtle about avoiding his asking questions about her family situation. There was so much about this woman he wanted to know. Especially who'd hurt her so deeply.

The week passed faster than Rebecca could imagine. Colby healed perfectly with a nice scar to show all the kids in kindergarten in the fall. Mitch got the herd into the feed lot and she toured the site for the slaughterhouse and meat-packing plant. Another six months and it would be up and operational. Mitch Tucker got things done, or he figured out a way to work around them.

The morning of her departure, Greta fixed breakfast while Rebecca packed her suitcases. After rechecking all the drawers to see if she'd forgotten anything, she headed to the kitchen. It was going to be tough to say goodbye. She wondered if she should even return here. Maybe it was better for everyone if she didn't. Cut her losses before someone got hurt, namely her.

She met Mitch in the kitchen, but he wasn't alone. He'd played the kid card, and both Colby and Greta looked adorable, and very sad that she was leaving.

"I don't want you to go, Rebecca," Colby said.

"But I need to be in my office for a while. I've been away for nearly three weeks." The children were others that could be hurt if she started something with their father, started a relationship that couldn't lead anywhere. She had no future with a man who wanted a houseful of kids.

After she hugged them both goodbye, Mitch helped her into the Range Rover. Then he instructed his daughter to watch Colby until he returned. He started the truck and pulled away. Rebecca watched the two kids waving, looking forlorn. Why did she feel she was abandoning them?

In a sudden moment of panic, Rebecca wanted to

call it off, reveal her feelings to Mitch and confide that she wanted to stay and see where this would lead. But she couldn't saddle him with her problem. She had to go this alone, as she'd had to do since she was a kid.

Mitch kept the conversation light until he pulled up at the landing strip. He climbed out and Wally gave him the thumbs-up from the Cessna that he was checked out to go.

Mitch wasn't ready to let Rebecca go. He helped her from the passenger side, but blocked her path until he said what he needed to say. "Think about us while you're gone."

"Of course, but, Mitch…" She closed her eyes a second. "When I come back, it has to be different."

He relented, realizing if he didn't, she might not return. "Okay, if that's what you want, I'll keep us business. But you agree that after we get this project going, we'll see what happens—where this can lead."

She didn't get a chance to answer. Wally came over, took her bags from the back and loaded them into the plane.

"I should go, so I can make my connection in Denver."

Finally he leaned down and kissed her, a soft kiss that offered tenderness. He pulled back. "Have a good flight, Rebecca."

"Goodbye, Mitch," she whispered and started for the plane.

He called to her and she turned. "Just so you know, whatever you're fighting, you don't have to go it alone. You have me."

After a week back in New York, Rebecca sat at her desk in her nice office. For years this had been everything to her. Her life. She'd worked day and night for it.

Now, all she could think about was how Colby and Greta were doing. How was Mitch handling the ranch and the kids? She shook away the thoughts. She had to stop this. What had happened in Wyoming was over. It was time to get back to reality.

Reality had hit her hard after she returned home. Yesterday had been the anniversary of her mother's death and she had been to the grave to find the flowers from her sister. Then today she'd received the phone call from Rachel asking if the roses had been placed at the graveside.

Rebecca wanted so badly to bridge the gap between them. But the call had ended before she could tell Rachel about the D and C the doctor had performed just days before, or that it was only a temporary solution. It wouldn't solve her problem. He'd wanted to schedule a hysterectomy in a few months.

Rebecca hadn't told her twin any of those things.

She would handle them as she always had, alone. Tears welled in her eyes as she thought about Mitch.

He'd always wanted a houseful of kids, he had said.

So how could Rebecca go back to Wyoming? She couldn't hide her feelings for Mitch…for his kids. And if something more developed between them, she couldn't handle his pity. He needed a younger woman who could give him a home, more children. That wasn't her.

There was a knock on the door, and Brent swung into the room, but he wasn't wearing his usual smile.

"Hey, Beck, we've got to talk." He sat down in the chair and stretched out his long legs.

"What's the problem?" she asked, taking her chair behind her desk.

"It all depends on what you define as a problem. How do you feel about returning to Wyoming?"

She tensed. "Come on, Brent. You know I can't." She hadn't revealed everything to her friend, but enough for him to know that things could easily stray from business. "I've committed my time to the Newman project. You promised you would finish the free-range beef project."

Brent raised a hand. "And I will—would, but Mitch Tucker has other ideas. He wants you and only you."

Rebecca breathed in and out to control her anger.

"He doesn't need me to finish this. I've done all the groundwork. Anyone can handle the rest."

Brent looked concerned. "Tucker has threatened to go to another agency if you don't return to finish the job."

Rebecca sucked in a breath. "Can he do that?"

"According to our legal department he can. Dad is adamant about this, Beck. He wants you to return to Wyoming."

Why was Mitch doing this to her? Maybe he was so used to getting what he wanted that he'd decided he wasn't finished with her. Well, she was finished with him. "Fine, I'll go, but I'm not happy being railroaded."

"Thanks, I owe you." He walked to the door and stopped. "Come on, Beck, it's only a few more weeks. When you get back home we'll celebrate."

"I may not survive till then," she murmured.

He arched an eyebrow. "I think you protest too much." He studied her for a long time. "If I didn't know better, I'd say this Wyoming cowboy was getting to you."

"That's crazy," she denied. Mitch Tucker had already gotten to her.

CHAPTER SEVEN

"OKAY, I'm back," Rebecca announced as she marched into the den and tossed her portfolio on the desk.

Mitch looked up at her, pretending he didn't care. But he did care. Very much.

He'd known Rebecca had landed thirty minutes ago but had decided to let Wally bring her to the house. He'd even asked Greta to help her get settled in her room, saying he had to take a conference call and couldn't be disturbed. There'd been no call. Not that Rebecca seemed to care if he were busy or not when she barged into his office.

"It's nice to have you back," he commented. But his eyes ate her up. He'd been starved for the sight of her this past week, not being able to see her every day. Even her black business suit worn like armor, and her beautiful hair pulled back and captured in a tight bun, didn't detract from her appeal. He had to fight to keep from coming around the desk and kissing her until she admitted how much she'd missed him, too.

His tactics to bring her back to Wyoming might have been a little underhanded, but desperate times called for desperate measures. He leaned back in his leather chair. "I want to continue moving forward on this project, and you and I worked together well."

She folded her arms "That's beside the point. You bullied me into coming back here. More importantly, you threatened my job at the Pierce Agency. It's my career."

Mitch worked to maintain his calm. He wasn't used to people questioning his decisions. "First of all, I would never threaten your career. I just didn't want to waste time bringing someone else up to speed."

Had he made a mistake about her feelings for him and his children? He knew he was taking a big risk, but hopefully it was worth it.

"Any one of my qualified associates could have handled your…needs. I would oversee things from New York."

At the sound of a horn, he glanced out the window to see the familiar school bus, then turned back to her. "Well, I'm the client here, and I want you on this project, and I want you here."

Rebecca reached for her portfolio. "Okay, let's get started…"

"Sorry, right now isn't a good time."

Her jaw tightened, revealing her irritation. "When would be a good time? I've prepared a presentation."

"It's going to have to be later today. No, tomorrow would be better. The kids are here to ride." He stood and started across the room, but paused. "If you're interested, I could use your help."

At his suggestion, her whole demeanor softened. "Of course, if you need me."

"Oh, I need you, all right," he said. "Later, I hope I get the chance to tell you—tell you how much it means to me that you've come back."

"You didn't give me a choice."

Even after changing into her jeans and boots, Rebecca still fumed over Mitch's arrogance. But as soon as she arrived at the corral and saw the kids her anger disappeared.

She was assigned to Matthew again. Today the boy let her take his hand and she walked him to Magic.

"I'm glad you came to ride, Matthew. Maybe today you can see if Magic will do some tricks."

"Magic," he murmured.

"Yes, you're going to ride Magic," Rebecca said, seeing his head was tilted toward the sun, a blank look on his face.

When she'd returned to New York, she'd done some research into the condition, learning that too many things going on at the same time could cause sensory overload. The autistic child withdrew or had a meltdown, indicating his anger or frustration.

Right now, Matthew seemed focused on getting on his horse. With some help from their spotter, Jimmy, Rebecca got the five-year-old in the saddle. She picked up the reins and they'd begun the journey around the corral when Mitch approached. He reassigned Jimmy and began to walk next to the horse.

"Hi, Matt." He patted the boy's leg.

"Hi, Mitch…"

Those dark brown eyes turned to Rebecca. "And how are you really doin'?"

She shrugged. "I can handle it," she told him. *It's you I can't handle,* she cried silently. "If you have to oversee other things, Matthew and I will be fine." Then she tugged on the rein and started off. She couldn't let this man get to her, but she knew he already had.

Mitch stared at her as he walked beside the horse. Rebecca Valentine had a big heart when it came to kids. He'd seen her share it with his children, and also with these kids. She fit in so well here.

She just didn't want anything to do with him.

Mitch motioned Jimmy to come back and spot for him. "I'll let you finish taking Matthew around." He checked his watch. "There's about another twenty minutes before we finish up." Before Rebecca said anything more, he strolled away.

Wasn't that what she wanted? For the man to leave her alone? She'd come here on business and as soon as she was finished she would return to New York and no one would get hurt. Her life would go back to normal.

Right. She closed her eyes for a moment. Nothing in her life had ever been normal. *Not when your family is named Valentine.*

Pushing aside her own problems, she smiled at Matthew.

"Okay, let's go." She tugged him toward the barrel in the middle of the corral, and the game began.

When the twenty minutes were up, Jimmy helped Matthew off the horse and Rebecca walked him back to the bus behind the other children.

One of the teachers took his hand. "Bye, Matthew," Rebecca said.

"Bye, Becca," Matthew called without looking at her.

Every time this child spoke to her, tears stung her eyes. Every small accomplishment was so huge.

Greta and Colby came up beside her. They waved as the bus pulled away and drove along the road until it disappeared from view.

"I'm glad you're back, Rebecca," Colby said. "I missed you."

"I'm glad I'm back, too." It was the truth. She'd missed these two kids more than she ever could have imagined. That was also one of the reasons she hadn't wanted to return. Leaving them again would only cause her more heartbreak.

She glanced toward the corral and saw Mitch walking toward them. His lazy swagger looked as if he had all day, but his six-foot-two height ate up a lot of ground. He was so appealing in those jeans and that fitted Western shirt, with a black cowboy hat sitting low on his forehead. Then he smiled at her. That all knowing, you're-crazy-about-me smile. She released a long breath. She was in deep trouble.

"Hey, how does everyone feel about pizza tonight?"

Colby jumped up and down. "Oh, boy. I love pizza."

"Me, too," Greta said.

They all turned to Rebecca. If she said no, then she was the bad guy. "Sure, pizza sounds good."

"Good," he said. "You kids go and get cleaned up."

Greta walked off with Colby, but Rebecca hung back to talk with Mitch. "I thought we were going to concentrate on the project."

"We will, but it's your first day back and the kids are tired of eating my cooking."

"Of course, but tomorrow I would like you to look over the artwork I've come up with."

He nodded. "Sure, I have the afternoon free." He studied her for a long time. "I missed you."

Rebecca felt a blush rise to her face. "Mitch, please," she begged. "I told you I can't work on this project if you make it personal."

"Rebecca, from the moment we met it's been personal between us."

"That doesn't mean we have to act on it. And you have Greta and Colby to think about."

That seemed to get to him. "Okay, maybe we should tread carefully, but first I haven't welcomed you back…home." He reached out and cupped the back of her neck and lowered his mouth to hers. Although the kiss was a mere brush of his lips against hers, the impact was still powerful. By the time he released her, she was dazed and breathless. A condition she was in a lot when she was around this man.

Rebecca rolled over in bed and glanced at the clock. It was after one a.m. and she couldn't sleep. Maybe that was because she'd slept in every morning until she knew that Mitch was gone from the house.

But she hadn't really slept. She'd heard all the sounds of a household waking up: Colby running down the stairs, Greta arguing with her brother, Mitch asking about breakfast. Rebecca had ached to join in, but that was a dream she dared not dream.

To stop her thoughts she got out of bed, slipped on a robe and walked to the kitchen. Relieved to have the solitude, she heated some water for tea, and then carried her cup and saucer into the sun room. She loved this part of the house. It was so cozy and private.

She sat down on the window-seat, breathed in the earth-scented night air and suddenly childhood memories of living with Poppy and Nana came to mind. Those days on the farm had been the best. For her and Rachel. They'd both been happy then. What had happened to them? Was her sister happy in England? Rebecca didn't even know that much about her twin. There was more than an ocean that separated them. That still separated them.

Rebecca sighed and took a sip of her tea. It wasn't that she hadn't wanted to resolve their problems, but over the years she had found it easier to put things off. She thought back to Rachel's phone call. She could sense that her sister had wanted to say more to her.

Now, after the e-mail she'd received from Stephanie earlier today, telling her of Grandfather William's poor health, she wondered if that was what Rachel wanted to tell her.

"Rebecca, are you okay?"

She swung around to find Mitch in the doorway. He was wearing a pair of black sweatpants and nothing else. His hair was mussed and she could tell he'd been in bed.

"I'm fine. I just got some tea, and was enjoying the peace and quiet."

He gave her a lopsided grin. "So you did miss what we have to offer when you went back to New York."

"I have to admit, I did." She stood, not wanting to deal with her feelings, or the look on his face. "I'll go back to my room."

"Please, I don't want to chase you off." He paused and raked his fingers through his hair. "I couldn't sleep, either. So why not keep each other company?"

She hesitated. "I could make you some of my tea."

"Cures all ills, huh?" He went to her, took her cup in his large hand and sipped. "Not bad."

The intimacy of his action sent her pulse racing. "A friend sends it to me from the UK."

"I don't think tea will solve my problem." He stared out into the starlit sky. "We've lost two calves this week."

"Oh, no. How?"

"The tracks show it's most likely a mountain lion."

She sucked in a breath. "A mountain lion."

"Don't worry. You and the kids are safe here. But the herd is vulnerable, so I've increased the night patrol."

"Will they catch it?"

He shrugged. "That would be nice, or if the cat would go back to feeding off the deer population. If not, we'll have to go after it."

Mitch didn't want to talk about cats; he was concerned about Rebecca. "What about you? What's got you up?"

"Oh, I was on the computer earlier." She sighed. "I just needed to unwind a little."

"Rebecca, you can't do business twenty-four seven."

"I was actually e-mailing my friend, Stephanie. It's difficult to call each other since she lives in London."

"It's good you stay in touch," he said, watching the dim light reflecting off her hair.

She smiled. "Stephanie and I have been friends since college. Whenever she comes to New York we get together."

"And since your family is in England, you must get to see her when you go there."

She glanced away. "I haven't been in a long time."

"What about your family? When do you see them?"

She hesitated a second. "When you're a product of divorce you don't always come out with a whole family. After our mother brought us to the States, we only went back a few times. Of course, Rachel returned to London after college. I decided to stay with our mother."

Mitch wanted to know everything about Rebecca. Just seeing the pain in her eyes and the loneliness in her voice tore him apart. Only his promise to her kept him from taking her in his arms. "What about after her death? You could have gone back…for a visit."

She shrugged and looked down into her almost empty cup. "By then I didn't feel like I fit in." Her voice was soft and hesitant. "Grandfather William always seemed to favor Rachel. Not that it was that obvious, but they've always gotten on so well."

Mitch's heart ached for her. How could anyone not love this woman? "What about your father?"

A half smile transformed her face. "Let's see…at last count, Robert Valentine has had a total of four marriages, and six children. The shame is, I don't think he's ever gotten over our mother. Diana Crawford Valentine was the love of his life."

"I'm sorry." He tried to reach out to her, but she stood and her teacup rattled as she moved away.

"Don't worry, Mitch. I got over my father's lack of interest a long time ago. I've made a life and career in New York."

He came toward her. "We don't get over needing family. If you had, it wouldn't bother you so much that you haven't seen your father and sister in— what…ten years?"

"We talk now and then," she offered. "We've just never been close."

Mitch didn't believe her casual attitude for a second. "Maybe after this project is finished, you can go see your friend, Stephanie, and let your sister know you're there."

He could see she was thinking about it. "So now you're a travel agent?" She laughed.

He smiled. "I'll even fly you over there."

She raised an eyebrow. "In your Cessna?"

"I also have a Lear jet in Cheyenne. Since I've retired I haven't used it much."

"Thank you for the offer, I'll consider it. I guess I should get to bed," she said as she started for the door.

"There's no need to run off." He came toward her. "I promised I wouldn't pressure you and I'll keep my word."

"I know." She swallowed. "I just need some sleep."

He took a step closer, getting into her space so he could inhale her sweet scent. "Darlin', I haven't been able to sleep since you came to Wyoming. And it's been the sweetest suffering I've ever endured."

The sweetest suffering I've ever endured.

The next morning, Rebecca tried to get some work done, but Mitch's words kept distracting her. She finally tossed her pen down on the desk and looked out the window.

That was when she saw Mitch. He was leading four saddled horses toward the house. The mounts were the same they'd ridden out to see the herd when she'd first arrived at the ranch.

Her attention turned to the two kids running out the door. Their father said something to them and Greta went back into the house. It wasn't long until she appeared at the office door.

"Rebecca," she said, "I know we're not supposed to bother you when you're working, but Dad, Colby and I want to know if you'd like to ride with us out to Horseshoe Pond. We're going swimming."

Rebecca found she was as excited as Greta. The last thing she wanted to do was stay here all day alone.

"I'd love to go." She came around the desk. "Just give me five minutes to change." Rebecca started out of the room, and Greta reminded her to bring a swimsuit if she had one.

Once in the bedroom, Rebecca dug through the pockets of her suitcase where she always packed a simple one piece suit to use at hotel pools. It took two extra minutes to put it on under her jeans and T-shirt. She grabbed her hat off the hook as she walked out the back door, and hurried down the steps. Colby and Greta were already on their horses.

Smiling, Mitch held out Ginger's reins to her. "I'm glad you could make it."

"Thanks for inviting me."

He suddenly sobered. "I planned this day for you, Rebecca. Just so you could see there are other things in life besides work. I plan to show you how to relax."

"Come on, Dad, Rebecca," Colby called impatiently.

Barely managing to tear her gaze away from Mitch's, she went to Ginger and swung up into the saddle. This time Greta took charge of her brother and they led the foursome along the path.

"You know we can only play hookey for so long," Rebecca said.

He smiled. "I'm the boss, so I say when we work. Besides, it's too nice a day to work. What will it hurt if we take a little break?"

It could be very dangerous, she thought.

He glanced up at the cloudless sky. "There's plenty of time during the Wyoming winters to hang around the house."

Rebecca felt a stab of regret. "I won't be here this winter."

He sighed and gave her a sideways glance. "I guess I'll just have to think up another project to keep you here."

What was he trying to do to her? "That would be an expensive endeavor."

His eyes locked with hers, stirring up all sorts of sensations. "You're worth it."

She didn't know how to answer, so she didn't even try as they continued to follow the trail.

Over the next twenty minutes Mitch kept it light with stories of his childhood. Rebecca talked about her time on the horse farm. There was such an easy banter between them that she was surprised to find they'd reached their destination. A group of trees at the base of the foothills sheltered a small pool of water.

Colby was the first to slip off his horse. "Dad, can we go swimming now?"

"Just let me take care of the horses." Mitch climbed off his mount and Rebecca followed. The summer sun had caused the temperature to climb and the water did look inviting.

Mitch took the horses to the edge of the pond for a drink, then into the shade and dropped their reins so they could graze. He untied the blanket from his saddle and with Greta's help, spread it on the ground.

The kids plopped down and quickly pulled off their boots, next came their T-shirts and jeans, revealing their swimsuits underneath.

"My dad used to swim here when he was a kid," Colby volunteered. "He skinny-dipped." The kid grinned. "That means he was naked."

"Too much information, son," Mitch said. He glanced at Rebecca. "You probably didn't have a suit with you… I wouldn't go in but there's a deep end to the pond and I need to play lifeguard."

Colby screamed as he jumped into the cool water. Mitch sat down and pulled off his boots, socks and jeans, revealing a pair of navy boxer-style trunks. "It's a shame you can't go in."

Rebecca felt giddy as she tugged off her boots and stood up. "But I hear you don't need a suit here." She unfastened her jeans and began to lower the zipper…slowly. She bit back a smile, seeing Mitch swallow as she tugged her pants downward. "I guess if you can skinny-dip, so can I."

The tables were turned as she saw a rush of excitement and desire in his eyes.

"You're playin' with fire, darlin'," he said in his best cowboy drawl. "If you want me to keep my hands off you, you'll need to cooperate." Slowly a wicked grin appeared. "No, on second thought, don't stop on my account."

Rebecca swallowed hard and her hand began to shake as she pushed her jeans off, revealing her long legs.

Mitch watched her every move. "Damn, if I knew you were hiding those beauties, I'd…"

Suddenly Colby called to him. He stood and yanked off his shirt. It was her turn to stare. The man was built, and she didn't think he'd been aided by any gym work.

"I'll meet you in the water," he told her, then ran off toward the kids. She watched as he picked up Colby and dunked the giggling child into the water.

Rebecca removed her blouse, and walked to the edge where Greta was waiting for her. Together they sank into the cool water.

Mitch's father had lined the bottom of the pond with rocks and sand, making it a nice place to swim. It took a few minutes, but Rebecca soon adjusted to the water and began to swim with Greta. Colby started making a commotion at the far end where there was a large tree and a long knotted rope. Mitch climbed out of the water, and, with his kids egging him on, he stood on a big rock and grabbed hold of the rigging. With a loud Tarzan cry, he swung out over the water, then let go and landed with a big splash.

Colby and Greta cheered their father's antics. But when he didn't surface immediately, Rebecca was worried, until she suddenly felt hands on her waist. She gasped as he raised her up out of the water and tossed her back in.

Rebecca came up sputtering. "That wasn't nice." She brushed her thick hair out of her eyes.

Mitch moved toward her. "I'm sorry. Are you okay?"

Catching him off guard, Rebecca used her leg for leverage, and shoved him backward into the water. He came up surprised, but smiling.

"So you want to play?"

"You started it." She backed away.

"And I always finish what I start," he said, moving toward her. "After that little striptease of yours…" he kept his voice low "…how do you expect me to keep my hands off you?"

She swallowed. "I didn't mean…"

Mitch was half mad for this woman. The simple nylon suit showed off every curve of her sexy little body. "Rebecca, you made me crazy just looking at you." His gaze wandered down over her curves. "In that suit you should be illegal."

She tried to move away, but he grasped her arm.

"Don't run away, Rebecca. I know you're afraid, but you can't deny what's happening any more than I can."

Tired of being ignored, Colby and Greta called to them.

Mitch knew he had to go. "This isn't the time or place to discuss this, but I'm not letting it go. Not unless you tell me to." He searched her face. "If you want me to stay away, I will, but I don't think it is what you really want."

"We can't always get what we want," she said weakly.

"Do you want me to kiss you right here and prove you wrong? I care about you, Rebecca Valentine. Now, I need some honesty from you."

Her beautiful blue-gray gaze widened, her breathing was ragged. He released the hold on her arm. "Say it, Becca."

She closed her eyes momentarily. "Okay. Yes! I care about you. I don't want you to stay away."

He smiled, and glanced toward his kids. "Just hold that thought until about nine o'clock tonight."

CHAPTER EIGHT

SHE was playing with fire and she might get burned.

Rebecca paced the sun room while Mitch was upstairs with Colby and Greta, making sure they were settled in for the night.

She clasped her hands together. She had no idea what Mitch expected from her when he came downstairs. No, that was a lie. Of course she knew. He wanted her…in the biblical sense. And she wasn't any good at this. The only two relationships in her life had consisted of one short-term boyfriend in college that had been the typical see-what-sex-is-like experience.

She hadn't been impressed.

Then, in her early years at the Pierce Agency, she had shared a brief fling with Brent during a business trip. Luckily, they'd remained friends after that disaster.

Now, there was Mitch Tucker. What category did he fit into? He'd been married for years. He was definitely a for-ever kind of guy. A family man.

She closed her eyes. If only he'd come into her life five years ago. Not now, not when her life was in turmoil. Not when she had to face a life-changing decision—and not with a man who wanted more children. That above everything else tore at her.

Her chest tightened with emotions she'd never felt before. "I could so easily love you, Mitch Tucker."

"Rebecca…"

She swung around. The man in question was standing in the doorway. He was handsome, sexy… with dark, piercing eyes that seemed to see right through her. A warm shiver moved down her spine as she remembered how it felt to have his skilled hands on her. A lazy smile curved his mouth and suddenly she couldn't breathe.

He walked toward her and drew her into an embrace. "Are you all right?" he murmured against her ear.

Unable to resist him, she wrapped her arms around his waist and snuggled into the welcoming warmth of his chest. "I'm not sure," she admitted. "But don't let me go."

Rebecca wished she could block out the world, but too many people were involved, including the two kids asleep upstairs.

"I wasn't planning to any time soon," he told her. He cupped her face and touched his mouth to hers in a whisper of a kiss so tender she felt light-headed.

How could being with Mitch seem so right and yet be so wrong?

Mitch needed to slow things down. He didn't want to push too hard. If he hadn't insisted that she return to Wyoming, she would be out of his life. That realization tore him up.

He pulled away, and rested his forehead against hers. "Rebecca, I'm trying to tread slowly with you… but when you're in my arms it becomes damn difficult." But, unable to help himself, he kissed her again. This time he showed her his hunger and she responded to him. His hands moved over her body, finally bringing her against him. With Rebecca it was more than a physical thing. He needed *her*. Her smile, her heart…

She broke off the kiss, her face flushed and her lips swollen. She stepped back. "Mitch…this is happening too fast…" Her shaky hand brushed back her hair. "We don't know each other…"

"Better than most, since we've lived in the same house for the past month," he insisted.

She arched an eyebrow. "Not the same thing. Besides, I'm going back to New York soon. You live here."

"Do you have to go back…right away?"

"Yes, my life, my career is there. Those things are important to me."

"I'm not asking you to give them up," he said

calmly. "Just take some time…to see about us. There are other things in life, Rebecca," he said. To prove it, he captured her mouth in another passionate kiss.

When he released her, she stumbled backward. "Is that your answer to everything?"

"If you were honest you would admit it's the same for you."

She groaned and turned away. "I can't do this."

"Do what? Just act on your feelings? Stop hiding behind your job, Rebecca."

Her eyes blazed. "I'm not hiding anything. I came here to do a job, and if that's not enough I can be gone in the morning."

"Rebecca, that's not what I meant. You're doing a great job," he said, but it was obvious that she'd already tuned him out.

The phone rang. Mitch cursed as he went to the table and grabbed the receiver. "Hello," he barked.

"Mitch, it's Wally. I'm sorry to bother you so late."

"Not a problem. What's up?"

"Neil just radioed in. We lost another calf."

"Damn." He turned away from Rebecca. "Did he see anything?"

"Yeah, he heard a commotion and got there just as a big cat took off toward the foothills above the south pasture. He also found some tracks. Charlie Peterson got hit, too. Last night. He wants to go after the cat—tonight."

"Okay, Wally. Get together a couple of the men you want to take with you."

He felt Rebecca's hand on his arm. "What happened?"

He covered the mouthpiece. "The mountain lion got another calf. Wally's going to take some men and go after it."

"What about you?" she asked. "Don't you need to go?"

He shook his head. "I can't leave Greta and Colby."

"You won't be leaving them alone. I'll be here."

He studied her. How could she say she didn't want to get involved when she already was? "It's not fair to ask you—"

"Is it fair that a mountain lion is killing off your herd?"

"I don't know how long I'll be gone," he told her.

"I'm not going anywhere."

But she was. She'd be leaving soon. Without taking his gaze from her, he removed his hand from the mouthpiece. "Wally, there's a change of plans. I'll be going along. Just give me ten minutes." He hung up. "Come on, we can talk as I get ready." He took her hand and pulled her along with him.

Rebecca wanted to refuse to go, but she suspected that Mitch wanted to instruct her about the kids. Together they climbed the stairs and walked down the hall through double doors that led into the master bedroom. Rebecca was taken aback as she glanced around at the soft green walls and plush ecru carpet. A dark armoire and dresser matched the straight lines of the king-size bed that was adorned with a rust-colored comforter.

It was definitely a man's room, except for the glow that came from the lit candles. She suddenly realized that he'd planned to bring her here.

Mitch quickly extinguished the burning wicks. He went to the dresser, pulled out a pair of jeans and a T-shirt, then went to the closet and took out a black sweatshirt. He dumped the clothes on the bed, then disappeared into the connecting bathroom. When he returned he was carrying a small case.

"I needed a toothbrush." He tossed the toiletries on top, then rolled up the clothes. His eyes met hers. "As you can see, I had different plans for tonight."

Rebecca didn't want to rehash what had happened between them. "It's better things didn't go any further."

He nodded. "Maybe. I don't think I need to instruct you on how to handle Greta and Colby. Just tell them I love them, and I'll be back as soon as I can. I'll have my cell phone. Call me if you need anything." He released a long breath. "Are you sure you want to do this?"

She nodded. "I'm sure," she said. "Now, you better get going."

For a moment they stood very still, staring into each other's eyes. When he came toward her, she held her breath. "You could sleep in here so you're close to the kids. Of course, I might not be able to concentrate on tracking the cat if I'm picturing you in my bed."

She wouldn't be able to sleep, either. "I'll just stay in my room and leave the door open. You should get going."

He reached for her. "I don't want to leave you, Rebecca. Not now, not when I need to convince you to give us a chance."

"Please, Mitch. You need to go."

"Then kiss me, Becca," he said in a low, husky voice. "Let me know that you'll miss me."

She rose up on her toes and pressed her lips gently against his, but Mitch wouldn't settle for gentle. Tipping her head back, he parted her lips to taste her. He caught her around the waist and tugged her roughly against him, letting her feel his desire.

When he released her, his dark gaze held hers. "Think about me when I'm gone." He kissed the tip of her nose. "I've got to go."

She nodded. "Be careful."

"Always," he said, then grabbed his things off the bed and headed for the door. "I had this room redone last year. You're the first woman who's been here. You're the first woman I've *wanted* here."

* * *

With Mitch gone the kids were handling the separation in different ways. Even though Greta tried to hide her fear with grumpiness, Rebecca knew the girl was worried about her dad's safety.

Colby was excited by the idea of his father being a hunter, and couldn't wait until he brought back a trophy.

And last night Rebecca had slept in her own room, but she'd been tempted to move to Mitch's bed if only to feel closer to him.

That would have been foolish. She had to keep reminding herself a future between them was impossible. They were too different. She lived in New York; he lived here. Her career was everything to her—the only staple in her life. She'd been able to depend on her work. It was what she fell back on when she had nothing else.

But that didn't stop her from dreaming of a family.

With her mother and Nana and Poppy Crawford gone, she didn't have any family close. Her blood relatives were in the UK, but they really didn't count. Her own father never had time for her—not once over the years had he asked her to come for a visit.

And Rachel. Rebecca knew she'd been partly to blame for their estrangement. Maybe she should have tried to repair the problems between them. They'd been apart for so long now. It was too late— too late for a lot of things.

She absently touched her stomach and thought about her condition. She had to concentrate on that rather than having a man in her life.

Mitch was going through a transition, too. He hadn't dated a single woman since his wife's death. A virile man like Mitch Tucker needed a sexy, exciting woman in his life.

Not…not half a woman.

She heard Greta's agitated voice and headed to the family room. Colby had a toy rifle and was pretending to shoot it.

"Get rid of that stupid rifle," Greta insisted.

"I don't have to," he argued. "I'm practicing so when I get older enough I can go hunting with Dad. I'm going to kill a wild animal and hang the head on the fireplace."

"That's gross. You're gross," Greta said. "Dad is only shooting the mountain lion because it's hurting our calves, not for a trophy."

"It's okay to hunt, Dad said, 'cause there's too many animals."

Greta jammed her fists on her hips. "You don't have to be so happy about it." Tears flooded her eyes. "You know Dad could get hurt…"

That took the air out of Colby's sails and he went to his sister. "Okay, Greta, I won't shoot my gun any more…in the house."

Rebecca crossed the room. "Colby, why don't

you go get your pajamas on and then you can watch a movie before bed?"

The boy grinned. It was already his bedtime. "All right," he cried and dashed out of the room.

Rebecca turned to Greta. "Honey, I know you're worried," she said. They all were. Rebecca had gotten a quick call from Mitch, just checking on the kids. "But your dad will be careful."

"I know, but what if the cat…?" The girl turned away.

Rebecca took Greta in her arms. "Your dad is with a dozen other men."

"I know, but he's all we have…"

Rebecca understood how the girl felt. "Not so. You have Margie, your grandparents in Florida, and Wally. And you have me." Rebecca found she meant that and wished it could be more. "Now, I don't want your father to come back and find your glum faces."

Greta looked up at her and smiled. "I'm glad you came to Wyoming."

"I am, too," Rebecca admitted, even though she would be leaving soon.

"I am too. What?" a familiar voice asked.

The three turned to find Mitch standing in the doorway. Rebecca ate up the sight of him. He looked tired and dirty, but no less than wonderful to her.

"Dad," Greta yelled and went running into his arms. Then Colby arrived to get a hug.

"Hey, Dad, did you kill the cat?" the boy asked.

Mitch was so glad to be home that he didn't want to go into the details of the hunt. He just nodded. "We didn't have any choice, son."

Colby jumped up and down. "Are you going to get it stuffed?"

"Colby, no." Greta folded her arms. "I'm not going to live in a house with dead animals."

"Neither am I," Mitch said and caught Rebecca out of the corner of his eye. She was wearing jeans and a rich blue Western-style blouse and looked as if she belonged here. He liked that.

"Hi, Rebecca," he said.

"Welcome back, Mitch."

"It's good to be back." His gaze moved to her hair. She wore it down in waves. He itched to get his fingers in the silky strands.

"I hope these two weren't too much of a handful."

"No, Dad. We were good," Colby said. "Rebecca took us into town and we got school stuff, and we had lunch at the café. And Greta wanted to buy a really short skirt, but Rebecca said it wasn't a good idea. That a girl needs to leave a little mystery." He wrinkled his nose. "What does that mean?"

Mitch couldn't help but smile. "I'll explain it in about ten years, son."

"We worked, too, Dad," Greta added. "We even talked about the idea for the kids' camp. Rebecca came up with the name Carrie's Camp. In honor of Mom."

Mitch's throat tightened. His deceased wife's dream, a reality. He looked at Rebecca. "It seems you've been busy."

"I thought the kids might like to be involved with the planning stage."

He wanted nothing more than to walk across the room and take this woman in his arms. Later, he told himself. "Kids, I think it's time you both should be in bed."

"But I want you to tell us about the cat," Colby begged.

"In the morning," Mitch said, unable to think about anything except being with Rebecca. "Greta, will you take your brother upstairs? I'd like to talk with Rebecca."

Greta glanced between the two adults, and smiled. "Sure, Dad. Come on, Colby." She tugged at her brother. "I'll read you a story."

Left alone, Mitch walked across the room toward the woman he'd thought about all during his time on the range. Now he was certain he wanted her in his life. "I missed you."

"I'm glad you're back…safe."

He took another step. "Since I've been away all I've thought about is…this…" He caught her head between his hands, leaned down and took her mouth. Hit with a rush of feelings, he nestled her closer, vowing to do whatever it took to keep Rebecca with him.

He finally broke away. "I have to smell like an old goat. I'm going to take a shower and say goodnight to the kids, then I'll be back so we can have some time together. I plan to convince you that we belong together."

Thirty minutes later, Rebecca still wasn't thinking clearly when there was a knock on her bedroom door. She answered it to find Mitch, clean-shaven, and his hair still damp from his shower.

When he took her in his arms he made her forget about common sense. And she'd always prided herself on thinking things through. But this man made her want to feel—feel his mouth on hers, his hands on her body.

He finally broke off a kiss, but didn't release her.

"I like the way you say hello." His dark eyes locked with hers. "If you only knew how much I missed you. How much I want you." He brushed his lips over hers, nibbling, tasting, teasing her. "Damn, I can't get enough of you. I don't want to let you go."

She hated herself for her weakness, but she couldn't let him go, either. Not yet. "I don't want you to," she confessed.

He froze and his gaze searched her face. "Be sure, Becca."

Rebecca blocked out everything but this night, and being with the man she loved this one time. She didn't want to love him but she couldn't deny her feelings any longer.

"I am sure."

The words were barely spoken when he captured her mouth in a demanding kiss, then released her to lead her into her room. Once the door shut, he leaned her up against it and his mouth came crushing down on hers again. His hunger was evident as he parted her lips and slid inside, deepening the kiss. It wasn't long before Rebecca was caught up in the sweet pleasure.

Mitch moved from her lips to her cheek, trailing kisses until he reached her ear. "You're driving me crazy, and I think you like that," he breathed. "Be warned, Becca, I'm going to return the favor." Then he proceeded to whisper in her ear how he planned to love her and she shivered.

Just this once, she told herself. Just once she wanted to know what it was like to love…and be loved.

Sliding her hands up his broad back, Rebecca pressed her breasts against his chest. "So far, you're all talk, cowboy."

That was all she got to say as Mitch swung her up into his arms and carried her across the room. He kissed her as he set her down on the floor next to the bed. "I'm going to make you pay for that."

Mitch felt raw as he cupped his hands under her chin, and tilted her head toward him. Inhaling unevenly, he covered her mouth with a soft, searching kiss. He drank from her, savoring the taste of her, trying to relay what she was doing to him, the feelings she drew from him. It had been so long since he'd felt anything like this, if ever.

He quickly worked the buttons on her blouse, then stripped it off her shoulders and let it drop to the floor. Her pale skin glistened in the dim light, and he hesitated to touch her, less he lost all control.

She tugged at his T-shirt, and he finished the job, pulling it off over his head. Then she reached out and ran her fingers over him. Next, he watched as her shaky hands unclasped the lacy bra and let it drop to the floor. "Love me, Mitch," she whispered. "Love me tonight."

He sucked in a breath. "I plan to, oh, Becca, I plan to." His mouth covered hers as he gathered her into his arms and pressed her back into the bed. Then he began to fulfill his promise.

CHAPTER NINE

JUST before dawn, Mitch lay on his side watching Rebecca sleep. Facing him, her hands tucked under her cheek, she looked so innocent. He wanted to wake her up and repeat what they'd shared throughout the night. His body stirred as he remembered how Rebecca had come alive under his touch. He preened a little, knowing how he'd pleasured her, and she'd returned it in so many ways.

Rebecca whimpered his name as she shifted in her sleep, and Mitch leaned down and placed a soft kiss on her lips. She didn't respond. So she wasn't so easy to wake up, he thought, recalling her need for morning coffee. He didn't give up easily and returned to her tempting mouth.

Rebecca arched into the warmth as skilled hands caressed her body, making her tingle. She wanted more. Fighting sleep, she blinked and tried to adjust to the dim light.

"Well, hello." Mitch's voice was low and husky.

She froze as their night together flashed in her head. "Mitch, what are you doing here?" she asked, a little too harshly.

He blinked. "I guess if you have to ask, I didn't make an impression." He sighed. "I'll just have to show you." He reached for her and she pulled away.

Sitting up, she bunched the sheet against her breasts. "I mean…I thought you'd be gone…because of the kids." Oh, Lord, she couldn't face him now.

"Greta and Colby are still asleep." He sat up, and the sheet fell to his hips, revealing that he was naked.

She turned away. Why hadn't she thought about the morning after? "Maybe you should leave anyway."

Mitch didn't move. "Becca, what's happening here? What's changed since last night?"

Everything! She was trembling. "It's just that I don't want to answer a lot of questions…from impressionable kids."

He didn't say anything for a long time, then she felt him get up and heard the sound of him pulling on his jeans. He came around the bed and handed her a robe. "Put this on, and we'll talk."

That was the last thing she wanted to do, but she didn't have a choice. She managed to slip on the robe, tie the belt, and move to the other side of the room. For what she had to say, she needed to be as far away from him as possible.

He spread his hands. "Did I do something wrong?"

She shook her head. "Oh, no…last night was wonderful." She couldn't believe how tender and loving he'd been with her. "But it can't happen again, Mitch. It wouldn't be wise. I'm returning to my life in New York, and you and the kids have your life here."

She couldn't catch her breath as she stared at the tall gorgeous man, his broad shoulders and chest and that slim waist. Wranglers hung on his slim hips, the top button undone. Desire shot through her.

"There's got to be some middle ground…some way to work it out. If we're both willing to give a little… To compromise…" He started toward her. "That's what couples do when they fall in love."

Oh, no, don't let him say love. Fighting tears, she held up her hand. "Please, Mitch. Don't make this difficult."

"Oh, darlin', I plan to make it very hard for you to leave me."

She had to get him out of there before she broke down. "Well, I'm not going to listen," she said as she started for the door and opened it. "You need to go. I refuse to argue with you about this."

He stood, rooted to the spot, then finally relented and headed for the exit just as the phone rang.

Mitch went to the extension in the hall and picked

up the receiver. "Hello," he said. "Yes, this is the Tucker Ranch. Yes, she's here. One moment please." He held out the phone to Rebecca. "It's your sister."

Rachel? Rebecca's heart raced. Why would Rachel be calling her? She took the receiver from him. "Hello, Rachel?"

"Rebecca, Stephanie helped me locate you. It's Grandfather William. I—I'm afraid he's dying."

She heard Rachel draw a breath. "He's asking for you, Rebecca."

Rebecca's chest tightened. It had been so many years since she'd seen her grandfather, but that didn't mean she didn't love the man. "He's dying?"

Rebecca tried to take it all in as her sister told her it was only a matter of time, and begged her not to miss this last opportunity to see him. Worse, Rebecca heard the tremble in her sister's voice as she revealed how much she regretted not being there when their mother died. "I should have been there, Rebecca. I should have been there for you, too. Don't miss this chance to say goodbye to Grandfather."

Rebecca could barely speak, let alone make a split-second decision. Then she felt a hand on her shoulder and turned to find Mitch beside her. He took the phone from her.

Not taking his gaze from her, he spoke the words she couldn't manage. "Rachel, this is Mitch Tucker," he said. "I'll make sure your sister gets on a plane."

He paused, listened, then looked at Rebecca. "Yes, she needs to be there with her family." He hung up, but only to make another call.

Rebecca walked back to her room in a trance. She closed the door, but that wouldn't keep Mitch out. How dared he make decisions for her? She knew she had to go to the UK, but how could she face the group of strangers who called themselves her family?

She needed someone with her. Taking her cell phone from her purse, she punched in Stephanie's number. After a minute or so she reached her close friend in London and informed her of her impending visit. Stephanie offered her a place to stay at her apartment. Rebecca promised to let her know when she would arrive at Heathrow Airport, and hung up.

There was a soft rap on the door, then it opened and Mitch walked in. "Rebecca, I don't think you should go alone," he said. "I want to go with you."

It took everything she had to shake her head as she pulled out her suitcase and began emptying out the dresser drawers. "No, I'll be fine," she said simply. She went into the bathroom and returned with her personal items. "This is my family. I'll handle it on my own." Right. Just as she'd handled everything so far, by simply ignoring it.

"Okay, but let me at least get you back to New York. I've already notified a pilot in Cheyenne. He'll bring the Lear jet here."

Before she could argue, Mitch left her to finish packing. It was better this way. The faster she got away from Mitch, the faster she could start forgetting him.

An hour later, Rebecca's bags were in the Range Rover and she was ready to leave. But was she? She was leaving Mitch and the kids. They were waiting for her outside. She slowly opened the door to see them lined up on the porch.

"I'm sorry about your grandpa, Rebecca," Greta said.

"Me, too," Colby added.

"Thank you." She hugged them both, then looked at Mitch. "I better get going."

"The plane is here." He opened the door.

She drew both children in her arms, desperate to hold back her tears. It was hard enough giving up Mitch, but these two… These children were her heart.

"I love you, Rebecca," Colby said.

"I love you, too," Greta echoed.

She was dying. "And I love you, back," she whispered over the lump in her throat as she hugged them both.

"Please come back soon," Greta pleaded.

Mitch stepped in. "Kids, Rebecca needs to catch a plane."

He escorted her to the passenger side, and walked around, climbed in and started up the truck. Surprisingly, Mitch didn't talk to her during the ride. He left her alone to look out the window at the mountains she'd come to know and love.

Finally they arrived at the air strip and Mitch parked. "Jerry Driscoll is my pilot. He'll get you to New York." He reached into his pocket and pulled out an itinerary. "I reserved a seat for you out of Kennedy with British Airways."

She wanted to argue that she could have made the calls, but she couldn't. "Thank you."

He helped her out while Wally took her bags from the back. Now all she had to do was leave Mitch and she'd be home free. "Thank you for everything. Goodbye, Mitch." She stole a glance at him. Bad idea.

He reached for her. "If you think I'm going to let you walk out of my life like this, you don't know me."

"Mitch, we've talked this to death," she said. "We're not right for each other."

"After what we shared last night, how can you say that?"

"I won't talk about this now." She glanced toward the small jet on the runway. She had to get away. "I need to leave."

But he still wouldn't let her go. "I can't let you go until you at least understand how I feel. I love you, Rebecca. Just give this a chance, we can make it work."

Her heart pounded hard. "We can't."

"You're wrong," he argued. "You love my kids. And I'd love nothing more than to be with you, to marry you, to have a child with you. Hell, I'd love to have a half-dozen more."

The pain was tearing her apart. "No, I can't do this."

"Why?" His eyes searched hers. "I've seen you with Greta and Colby and the way you treat Matthew. I know you care about them." He lowered his voice. "Becca, you were meant to have children."

There was another sharp pain that tore through her heart, nearly staggering her. "Just let me go, Mitch. Please…"

"Then tell me why you wouldn't give us a chance?" He kept at her. "Tell me why not?"

Finally the tears broke loose and ran down her face. "Because, Mitch, I can't have your baby! I can't have any man's baby."

She backed away when she saw the shock on his face. He finally started toward her and she couldn't stand to hear the regret or pity in his voice. "Oh, Rebecca…"

The pain was worse than she ever could imagine. "I've got to go. Goodbye, Mitch."

Rebecca turned and took off running. She didn't stop until she got onto the plane. Once the jet took off, she gave in and sobbed her heart out. She'd gotten the truth out. And she had finally gotten Mitch Tucker out of her life. For ever.

Now if she could just get him out of her heart.

The next morning, Rebecca handed the fare to the taxi driver and climbed out in front of the black wrought-iron fence surrounding William Valentine's white Georgian villa in London.

She stood on the sidewalk, exhausted. She hadn't slept in what felt like days. First that flight to New York, then racing to her apartment where she'd re-packed her suitcase, grabbed her passport, and headed out to the airport to catch her flight into Heathrow. Stephanie had met her, and after she'd dropped her bags off at her friend's apartment and freshened up, she'd come here.

Rebecca's grip tightened on the book in her hand. *Sleeping Beauty*. Grandfather William had presented Rachel a copy of *Black Beauty*, and she'd received a copy of *Sleeping Beauty* when they'd left London to move to the States over twenty years ago.

Before she'd left her apartment in New York, she'd found herself reaching for her favorite fairy tale, and reading as she'd crossed the Atlantic. It also saddened her that it had been so long since she'd seen her grandfather and had spent so many years away from a place that had once been her home.

Rebecca stepped through the gate and walked toward the huge double doors. She lifted the knocker and dropped it against the brass plate. The door was opened by an attractive, smiling middle-aged woman.

"Miss Valentine, it's so good of you to come. I'm Margaret Jordan. I work for your grandfather. Please come in, your sister is expecting you."

"Thank you, Margaret," Rebecca said and followed the woman inside. Suddenly childhood memories began to bombard Rebecca.

The floor of the grand entry hall was made up of large squares of marble tiles. The room was painted a deep taupe and trimmed with decorative bright white moldings and original artwork lined the walls. To her right was the formal parlor, painted in a sky blue with huge windows and high ceilings. A grouping of oversized furniture was centered in front of the fireplace.

Margaret waited for her at the bottom of the carpeted staircase, while overhead a crystal teardrop chandelier hung overhead from the twenty-foot ceiling.

She couldn't take it all in. More memories came as her hand moved over the carved handrail along the winding staircase. At the top, Rebecca hesitated. She and Rachel had played hide and seek here, going in and out of the many rooms. There also had been the special room Grandfather had decorated and filled with toys for his grandchildren.

A deep sadness overtook her thinking of William Valentine dying. She should have come back sooner. She should have had the chance to get to know her grandfather as an adult.

Margaret stopped at her grandfather's bedroom. She gave Rebecca a gentle smile. "He'll be so happy to see you." She knocked and opened the door.

Rebecca's pulse raced. She drew a calming breath, moved into the dim room and directed her gaze to the bed, at the frail man under pristine-white sheets.

Holding vigil next to the bed was Rebecca's twin, her beautiful sister. Rachel was tall and elegant, the picture of the professional woman with her dark brunette hair combed in a sleek style just brushing her shoulders. Rachel turned toward her and surprise and joy registered in her blue-gray eyes. She held out her hand.

All at once the years melted away, and Rebecca saw the loving look, mixed with some regret for all the lost years. She walked toward the bed and reached across for her sister's outstretched hand. They held tight to each other as if gathering strength for what was to come.

Rachel leaned closer to the thin man lying in the bed. An oxygen tube threaded through his nose.

After a moment her grandfather's eyes blinked open. Seeing the familiar steel-gray eyes, she smiled. "Hello, Grandfather."

William Valentine's gaze found Rachel, then Rebecca. Tears poured down his withered cheeks. "God heard my prayers. My two beauties together at last."

Rebecca stood on the white-railed balcony that over-looked Hyde Park. Stephanie's apartment above the Bella Lucia was a fringe benefit of her job as man-ager of one of London's finer restaurants. It was the second of three that the Valentine family owned in the area, all having been named after the love of her grandfather's life, his second wife, Lucia.

It seemed as if most family members worked in the business. Rachel was the wine buyer. Her half-sister, Emma, was a chef. Her father, Robert, and her half-brother, Max, managed the charter restaurant in Chelsea. Her uncle, John Valentine, managed the one in Mayfair. Now that Grandfather was gone, who would keep the peace between the rival brothers?

Rebecca had been ten years old when she'd left London, yet it seemed like yesterday. Except her grandfather had died, and he'd been buried just the day before. Thankfully she hadn't had to handle it on her own. Rachel had been there for her.

Suddenly, her thoughts turned to Mitch, as they had so many times since leaving Wyoming. And like the other times, she tried to push away all memories of the man. She couldn't deal with them right now.

Healing her relationship with her sister was her number one priority, and that had begun when she and Rachel had left Grandfather's sick room and taken the time to sit down and talk. Talk about the insecurities that their parents' divorce had caused. How they had both thought they had to choose sides, and in the process they had lost each other. Now they'd finally found each other again Rebecca was not going to let this chance get away from them.

Rebecca heard Stephanie's voice behind her and turned to smile at her friend. "How are you feeling?" she asked Rebecca.

"I'm fine."

Stephanie was tall and slender with wild red hair she continually tried to tame. There were very few people who knew the secrets behind those green eyes, or all the physical and emotional pain she had endured in her short life.

"Emma is bringing us lunch over from the restaurant."

Rebecca sighed. "I haven't had much of an appetite, but I'd like to spend time with her."

Emma was another family member Rebecca barely knew. Her younger half-sister was her father's daughter from Robert's marriage to his third wife, Cathy, a marriage that had ended the same year Rebecca's mother had died.

Stephanie nodded. "She's nice, and a fabulous chef for Bella Lucia."

"Then I look forward to sampling her food."

They both walked back into the spacious apartment. It was decorated with oriental influences, and contemporary art hung on the gold-colored walls. In the dining area, there were four place settings. Before she could ask about the other guest the bell rang and Stephanie opened the door to both Emma and Rachel.

A cheerful Emma carried the food containers into the apartment. "I talked our sister into coming, too," she said.

Rachel smiled, but Rebecca saw the sadness behind her sister's high spirits. Grandfather's death had been difficult for her. They'd been so close.

"I'm glad you did." She hugged her twin. "We've all been through a lot, and it's time we enjoy some time together before I have to leave."

"Oh, no, please tell me you aren't going back to the States so soon?" Rachel pleaded.

"I can't stay much longer; I have a job," Rebecca said. But did she? She'd walked out on the Tucker account. Told Mitch she wasn't coming back, and she hadn't really had a chance to talk to Brent since.

They all sat down and had a great lunch, but kept the conversation light. Eventually, Emma left to go back to the Bella Lucia in Chelsea and Stephanie disappeared into her bedroom, leaving the sisters alone.

"Rachel, I hate to see you so…down," Rebecca said. "How are you feeling?"

"I'm fine." Rachel brushed away her concern.

"Have you thought about what we talked about that day at Grandfather's?"

Her sister lowered her eyes. "I really haven't had much time to…" She got up and walked out onto the balcony.

Rebecca followed her. She had to tread gently, but didn't want Rachel to brush this away. Her sister had confided that she'd fallen in love with a French wine-maker, Lucien Chartier, and she was carrying his child.

"Rachel, I know that I haven't been there for you in the past, but I'd like to help now…with the baby."

Tears welled up in Rachel's eyes. "Oh, Rebecca, I've made such a mess." She broke down. "I love a man who…doesn't love me back."

Rebecca wrapped her arm around Rachel's shoulders and held her as she sobbed. She felt her sister's misery as deeply as if it were her own. "Has he told you that?"

Rachel shook her head. "No, but Luc's mother says he's still in love with his ex-wife." She dabbed at her eyes.

"His mother shouldn't interfere in this; she doesn't speak for Luc. It's between you and him. You need to make some plans."

"I know, and I have." She wiped away her tears. "I'm going to leave my position at Bella Lucia. I can't work with Father any longer. So, I need to ask you for a favor… I want to come to New York and look for a job managing a restaurant." She smiled hesitantly. "Would it be possible to stay with you for just a while?"

Emotions clogged Rebecca's throat. "Oh, Rachel, I'd love to have you stay with me." She gripped her sister's hands.

"Are you sure?" Rachel asked. "I know this is going to be difficult for you."

The day she'd arrived in London, Rebecca had updated her sister about her own medical problems. "Not as much as losing you again. This baby is a blessing. You and your child are welcome to stay with me for as long as you like. I want to be a part of my niece's or nephew's life."

Yes, Rebecca thought. She would need family with her, because she wouldn't have Mitch. Fresh thoughts of him rushed through her head of their night together. How she wished for some kind of miracle, a miracle that she had been able to conceive his child. It was natural that he would want more children. She just wished she could be the one who gave them to him. She couldn't.

Rebecca pulled herself out of her reverie. "Rachel, there is one condition before you come to

New York. You have to tell Luc. He deserves to know about his child."

Her sister paused, then finally nodded. "We've certainly gotten ourselves into messes, haven't we?" she said. "But here we are. We found each other."

They hugged.

Rachel pulled back. "Okay, now what about you?" she asked. "You're ready to hand out advice, but you're not taking any. You need to talk to Mitch, too."

Rebecca shrugged. "My situation is different. He's not my man."

Her sister didn't look convinced. "We're talking about the man who flew you to New York in his private jet. And the same man who answered the phone at the ranch and within seconds put you on the line. You two were in pretty close proximity at five in the morning…for him not being your man."

She sighed. "Okay, I let things get out of hand. And I fell in love with Mitch, but I can't burden him with my problem."

Rachel's look showed concern. "Seems you did the same thing I did. You ran away."

Rebecca frowned. "All right, I did. But he wants more children and when I told him I couldn't have any, he let me walk away." She fought her tears, but lost.

The sisters embraced again. "I wish there was something I could do to help."

Rebecca pulled back. "I'm fine, really. We'll both get through this, because we have each other again."

Just then Stephanie appeared in the doorway. "I hate to interrupt, but your father just called. He wants Rebecca to go to Grandfather's home."

Rebecca wasn't crazy about spending time with her father, any more than he was with her. "Did he say why?"

Stephanie raised an eyebrow. "It seems there's a Mr Mitchell Tucker waiting to see you."

CHAPTER TEN

MITCH sat in the large sitting room at William Valentine's home. He'd been waiting too long, and was impatient to see Rebecca. He'd resisted coming until her grandfather's wake and funeral were over before he flew to London to pour out his heart to her. Now, he had only a short time to find the words to convince Rebecca of his love. Let her believe that they belonged together. He refused to leave London without her.

Mitch got up and began to pace. For some reason Robert Valentine had decided his daughter's guest needed company. Of course it was the courteous thing to do, but Mitch knew too many things about Rebecca's father to want to be anything more than civil to the man. And after years in the corporate world, Mitch could see right through an opportunist.

"As I've told you, Mr Valentine, I'm no longer associated with Tucker International. I sold all my assets over two years ago. My family and the Tucker ranch is what I concentrate on now."

Robert Valentine was a tall man with black, brooding eyes, and hair just as black with a sprinkling of gray. He raised an eyebrow. "A man never leaves the corporate world. I hear you are in free-range beef now. Our restaurants just may be interested in doing business."

The last thing Mitch wanted to do was talk business right now. He had to see Rebecca. Nothing else mattered.

"It's going to be a while before we're operational," he told Valentine.

"Then we'll need to keep in touch." Robert smiled. "Since you are…working with my daughter—"

"Mr Valentine," Mitch interrupted. "My trip here has nothing to do with business. My reasons for wanting to see Rebecca are personal. And until I speak to her, I don't really give a damn about much else." He drew a calming breath. "So, please, don't let me take you away from your busy schedule."

Robert opened his mouth to say something when the sound of voices echoed from the entry. Anxiously, Mitch looked toward the doorway and froze when Rebecca appeared. He searched her face. She looked tired, yet beautiful. Her usually wild, sun-kissed brown hair was secured into a bun, but some wayward curls still had escaped. She wore a navy skirt that showed off her long legs and a blue sweater that brought out her eyes. He tried to gauge her reaction to his coming to London. She wasn't smiling.

"Hello, Rebecca," he said.

"Mitch, what are you doing here?"

Not what he wanted to hear, but what did he expect? He'd let her walk away when she'd dropped the bomb about her inability to have children. The news had broken his heart. Not for himself, but for her.

"I came to see you," he told her as he searched her face. Right now, he'd sell his soul to see her smile. "I was worried about you. The last time we spoke…"

She glanced at Robert. "Father, would you excuse us, please?"

Robert nodded, and said, "Why don't you go out to the garden? It's such a lovely day."

Rebecca recognized that familiar gleam in her father's eyes. A man like Mitch Tucker was someone that—despite the fact he was an American—Robert would consider a good prospect for his daughter, and for the Valentine family.

"Fine," she said, not caring where they went. She just wanted to get this over with. Somehow, she had to make Mitch leave. Then, and only then, she could begin to move on with her life.

On the way over to her grandfather's she'd practiced what she would say, but she'd had no idea that seeing him again would cause such an impact on her emotions. She couldn't remember a single thing.

The already handsome man looked even more so in his navy pinstripe suit with a snowy white shirt and burgundy tie. His hair was cut and styled perfectly, like the man himself. *Just get this over with and he'll leave.*

She crossed the room to the French doors, praying she could get through this. She opened the doors and stepped into the fragrant garden. There were dozens of colorful tea rosebushes lining the slate-covered terrace. As a child she had come here and many times walked the maze of stepping stones through the flowers, counting each one.

She shook away the memory. "Mitch, you shouldn't have come."

He followed her. "Oh, yes, Rebecca, this is where I should have been all along. I never should have let you handle all this on your own. If it weren't for the kids, I would have climbed on the plane with you."

She closed her eyes momentarily. "No, Mitch, we've said all we have to say. I'm not coming back to Wyoming. Nothing you say is going to change my mind, not even if it costs me my job at the agency."

He frowned. "Do you really believe I would cause you to lose your job?"

She could see she'd hurt him. "No, you wouldn't.

But we can no longer do business together. I'll give your account over to someone else."

"If that's what you want." He sighed. "It's a shame since you've put in so much work on the project. I've looked over more of your ideas, especially the one for Carrie's Camp."

"How did you know…?"

"I found your portfolio in my office. I figured you wanted me to see it."

She was shocked that she'd forgotten something so important to her. "Well, you paid for it."

"I paid for your ideas on my business endeavor." His gaze locked with hers. "What we shared that last night together was very special to me. I thought it was for you, too." He stepped closer and she backed away.

"Of course it was, but it's over," she said. "I'm going back to New York."

"What if I asked you to return to Wyoming again?"

It seemed as if her heart stopped, then it began to race. "Mitch, we've been through this. Our lives are too different. I have my work."

"Will you stop hiding behind your job? I'm not buying that act any more."

"It's not an act," she argued, but she knew it wasn't convincing. "I've worked hard to make a career."

"I don't doubt that, Rebecca. At one time I did too,

but I discovered that my wife and kids were more important. I think if you had a choice, you'd pick a family, but you think you can't have that. I'm here to convince you otherwise."

Rebecca felt a huge lump lodge in her throat. "I told you when I left Wyoming… I can't…" She turned away. "Please, don't put me through this again. Just go."

"Why should I make it easy for you? You're making things damn difficult for me. I came all this way to tell you that I love you. That my kids love you. And you won't even look at me."

Her chest grew painfully tight, but he was persistent as he took her by the arm and turned her around to face him. His eyes were dark and searching.

"I love you, Becca," he breathed. "I never thought I could care for another woman…" He took a breath. "When Carrie died I wanted to die. I pulled myself together and went on because of my kids. Then you walked into my life." He lowered his head, brushed his mouth against hers and heard her gasp.

"This isn't fair, Mitch." She wanted what he offered, even ached for it, but she was sure he would resent her later. "I only want you to have your dream."

"Rebecca, you are my dream."

She raised her eyes to meet his dark gaze. "But you…want more children. A houseful."

He pressed his forehead against hers. "Yes, I

wanted you to have my baby, but that would have been a bonus. It's you I want. You I need in my life…in my kids' lives. I want to grow old with you."

"But—"

"Don't interrupt," Mitch said. He was doing everything he could to convince her how much he loved her. "I love you so much, Rebecca. And I know you love me, too, or you never would have let me make love to you."

"That was wrong."

"No, it was right. We belong together." He pulled her into a tight embrace, dipped his head and covered her mouth with a long, searching kiss. When he came up for air, they were both breathless.

"I could kiss you for ever," Mitch breathed. "And it's distracting me." He took her hand and led her to a small wrought-iron bench in between the roses. "Tell me about your medical problem. Why is it you can't conceive?"

Mitch placed an arm around her shoulder and drew her against him as she explained about her endometriosis from adolescence and her prognosis for the future. "I have to return to New York and schedule surgery," she ended.

"Well, you aren't going alone. I'm going with you. But first we're getting a second opinion."

She raised her head. "Mitch, that's just it—I can't let you get your hopes up."

Mitch cupped her face. Somehow he had to make her realize how important she was to him. "I love you, Rebecca Valentine. Of course, I'd love to give you a child, but you are all I need. As for children—I know they aren't babies, but there are two kids in Wyoming who want you to be their mom." He felt tears sting his eyes. "They made me promise to bring you back."

"Oh, Mitch…if I thought for a minute that…"

"Rebecca, all you have to do is tell me you don't love me or my kids, and I'll walk out the door and you'll never see me again."

When she tried to look away, he grasped her chin. "I know a lot of people have let you down in your life, but I'm not going to. I promise I will be there for you, Becca. Always. Just tell me that you want me with you, that you love me." He needed to hear those words more than he needed air to breathe.

"I do," she whispered. "I love you, Mitch. So much."

"I'm glad that's settled." He slid off the bench and down on one knee. "Rebecca Valentine, I want nothing more than for you to do me the honor of being my wife and the mother of my children."

With a shaky hand, Mitch reached into his suit jacket and pulled out a velvet box. He opened it to reveal an antique-styled ring with a three-carat, round diamond in a platinum setting.

"Oh, Mitch," Rebecca gasped. "It's exquisite. I've never seen anything so beautiful."

He removed the ring from the box. "Give me your hand, Rebecca. Trust in my love for you. Starting now." He waited, his heart pounding so loudly he thought the world could hear. "Let's be a family."

She trembled as she placed her hand in his and he slipped the ring on her finger. "A perfect fit." He looked at her. "Just like we are." He stood, drew her into his arms and kissed her. When he broke off, he asked, "Is there anywhere we can go to be alone? I want to show you how much I've missed you."

She pulled away with a smile. "I'm afraid that isn't possible. You are marrying a woman with a rather large family. And I bet my sisters and my father are standing on the other side of that door wanting to know your intentions."

He grinned. "I'll tell them my honorable ones and then we can make our escape. Boy, a wedding better take place soon."

At the word "wedding" she bit her lip.

"It's going to be okay, Rebecca. We're going to have a wonderful life together," Mitch said. "We'll even work in some time for your career."

"My career isn't as important as you and the kids. Of course, I want you guys to continue sharing the chores."

Mitch leaned in and brushed his mouth against his future bride's. "That's all up for negotiation."

She placed her arms around his neck. "I have a feeling there's going to be a lot of negotiating in this marriage." She placed her mouth against his and began working on the terms.

EPILOGUE

Less than two hours before her wedding, Rebecca was in the master bedroom at the ranch trying to remain calm. Her sisters, Rachel and Emma, along with Stephanie, had flown in to be here for her special day. Over and over again they'd told her they were going to handle everything. Rebecca hadn't realized how much work it was to put on a wedding. Even holding it at the ranch, with less than a hundred guests, there was a lot to do.

Mitch wanted her to have this day. Rebecca wouldn't have cared if they went to a judge, as Rachel and Luc had done.

Rebecca studied the beautiful diamond that Mitch had given to her in London. Who would have thought when she'd left New York in May that she'd be having her wedding within the year.

She glanced at her dress lying on the bed. It was a copy of her Grandmother Lucia's wedding gown.

She ran her hand over the antique white satin with the intricately beaded scalloped neckline. When Mitch discovered how much she loved her grandmother's dress, he'd had a designer recreate it for her.

Rachel came in dressed in her rose pink bridesmaid's dress, her stomach protruding slightly with her pregnancy.

"How are you feeling?" Rebecca asked her sister.

"Stop worrying, I feel fine. I just wish you and Luc would stop asking every five minutes."

"We don't want you to overdo things." Rebecca was glad that her sister was so happy. It had turned out that Luc did love Rachel and had been eager to marry her, though it had just taken a few weeks for the stubborn Frenchman to confess his true feelings for her.

Rebecca would always be grateful that Mitch had been willing to risk coming for her, to convince her that they belonged together. And Greta and Colby had welcomed her with open arms. Oh, yes, she was lucky beyond belief.

Emma walked in. "Rebecca, I'm sorry, but it looks like Father isn't going to make it." Her younger sister traded glances with Rachel. "He just called to say something came up."

"Oh…" was all Rebecca could manage to say. She'd never asked much of Robert Valentine, but she'd thought that he would at least make it to her wedding.

A familiar nausea suddenly hit her. She ran into the connecting bathroom to be sick. Rachel and Stephanie helped her clean up and back into the bedroom.

"Don't let Father get to you," Rachel offered. "He's done this all our lives."

"It's just nerves," Rebecca said. "It's been going on all week. I can't wait until the wedding is over and my life gets back to normal."

Once again, Rachel and Emma exchanged a look.

"What?" Rebecca asked.

"This has been going on all week, you say?" Rachel asked. "Anything else, like…are your breasts tender?"

"Why, yes, they are, but…" Her heart skipped a beat as she thought about the possibility. "No… I can't be…pregnant. The doctor said that the scar tissue…"

"We need a pregnancy test," Rachel said.

Rebecca jumped up. "I can't take a pregnancy test. I'm getting married in an hour."

Mitch adjusted his tie again and smiled as he greeted the arriving guests, then he checked his watch. It should be about time to start. He was still angry to learn that Robert Valentine wasn't coming, only because he wanted this day to be perfect for Rebecca. Thinking about his bride, he smiled. How did he get so lucky to find her?

"Hey, Dad," Colby called as he tugged on his hand. "Is it time to get married yet?"

"Soon, son," Mitch said. "This is the bride's day and she may be running late."

"She's not going to change her mind, is she?"

"No, she isn't." He knelt down to his son's level. "What's bothering you, Colby?"

"I was just wondering if it's okay if I call Rebecca Mom. I mean she is, kinda…"

"Son, I think that will make Rebecca real happy. She loves you and Greta so much. She just wants you to be sure it's your choice."

His big brown eyes widened. "I decided I want to. You think I should ask her first?"

"How about right after the wedding?"

"All right!" Colby cried and high-fived his dad.

Mitch looked up. Stephanie and Emma were coming toward him. "Sorry about the hold-up, but we're ready now, so everyone should take their places." Emma smiled. "The bride needs an escort. Colby, how would you like to walk Rebecca down the aisle?"

Colby puffed out his chest. "Sure!" he crowed, and took off with the bridesmaids.

The guests sat in rows of white wooden chairs along an ivy-trimmed aisle. A white runner made a path for the bride. Mitch and his best man, Wally, stood next to the minister as the bridesmaids came toward them, a beautiful, beaming Greta leading the way. The music changed and everyone stood as Rebecca appeared with Colby.

Her gown was simple. The antique-white satin draped over her shapely body, tucked in at her waist, then flowed into a circle skirt to the floor, with a train in the back. It was an elegant nineteen-forties-style dress. Perfect for her. Perfect for his bride.

Her hair was pulled back with a ring of flowers woven through the strand and her veil was attached at the base of her neck. She carried a bouquet of pink roses. When she smiled Mitch's heart swelled.

They made their way up the aisle to him, and Colby gave Rebecca's hand to his dad. "She said yes, Dad," he whispered. "Rebecca said she'd love to be my mom."

That brought some chuckles from the guests as Colby took his place next to Greta. Mitch couldn't take his eyes off his bride. "You are beautiful."

"You don't clean up so bad yourself, cowboy."

He wanted to kiss her right there, but instead he tucked her arm in his and they turned to the minister.

Twenty minutes later, they were pronounced husband and wife. Mitch got his wish and pulled Rebecca in his arms and kissed her. He didn't release her until applause from the guests reminded him they weren't alone. They made their way up the aisle together.

After stealing another kiss, he whispered, "Hello, Mrs Tucker."

"Hello, Mr Tucker." She smiled. "Would you

mind coming with me before we head into the reception?"

"Haven't I proven I'd follow you anywhere?"

While everyone else headed to the patio, Rebecca took Mitch by the hand and led him to the sun room. When they closed the door, he pulled her into his arms and kissed her again.

"This is a great idea, but everyone is going to notice we're missing and come looking for us."

"I just wanted to give you your gift before we got too wrapped up in the reception. I couldn't wait," she admitted. She went to the table and picked up a small box tied with a simple bow.

He peered into her face. She was flushed and nervous. "You know I'm going to love anything you get me."

"Well, this is something we both wanted, but didn't plan on."

He pulled off the bow and opened the box to find a long white plastic stick. He recognized what it was immediately. And in the stick's window was a pink +. His heart raced. "You're pregnant?"

Rebecca trembled as she nodded. "I've been sick all week and Rachel said I needed to take a test. I called my doctor in New York. He said it was possible. That was why the ceremony was late getting started," she went on. "Emma drove into town to buy a test. I had to be sure." She sank into the window-seat. "I know this is a shock. We didn't plan this."

When Rebecca saw Mitch's grin she relaxed a little. He came and knelt down in front of her. "I'm just amazed. We spent one night together…and we made a baby." He blinked away the tears. "I'm humbled, to say the least."

She wanted so much to give Mitch a child. But was he ready for parenthood right now? "But happy?" she asked.

He gathered her into his arms. "My Becca," he breathed. "I don't even have the words to express what I'm feeling at this moment. I didn't think I could love you any more than I did, but I do…and I already love our child." He kissed her tenderly, gently, but with even more fervor. She'd never felt so cherished in her life. When he released her, he rested his head against her forehead.

"Let's not tell the others for a few weeks," she said. "I want to keep this just for us for a while." Tears glistened in her eyes as she touched her stomach. "This is our miracle."

"Our love is the miracle."

Rebecca knew the real miracle had been finding Mitch, and the family she'd always dreamed of.

SAVE UP TO $30! SIGN UP TODAY!

INSIDE *Romance*

The complete guide to your favorite
Harlequin®, Silhouette® and Love Inspired® books.

✓ Newsletter ABSOLUTELY FREE! No purchase necessary.

✓ Valuable coupons for future purchases of Harlequin,
  Silhouette and Love Inspired books in every issue!

✓ Special excerpts & previews in each issue. Learn about all
  the hottest titles before they arrive in stores.

✓ No hassle—mailed directly to your door!

✓ Comes complete with a handy shopping checklist
  so you won't miss out on any titles.

- -

SIGN ME UP TO RECEIVE INSIDE ROMANCE
ABSOLUTELY FREE
(Please print clearly)

Name

Address

City/Town   State/Province   Zip/Postal Code

(098 KKM EJL9)

Please mail this form to:
In the U.S.A.: Inside Romance, P.O. Box 9057, Buffalo, NY 14269-9057
In Canada: Inside Romance, P.O. Box 622, Fort Erie, ON L2A 5X3
OR visit http://www.eHarlequin.com/insideromance

IRNBPA06R   ® and ™ are trademarks owned and used by the trademark owner and/or its licensee.

Page-turning drama…

Exotic, glamorous locations…

Intense emotion and passionate seduction…

Sheikhs, princes and billionaire tycoons…

This summer, may we suggest:

THE SHEIKH'S DISOBEDIENT BRIDE
by Jane Porter

On sale June.

AT THE GREEK TYCOON'S BIDDING
by Cathy Williams

On sale July.

THE ITALIAN MILLIONAIRE'S VIRGIN WIFE

On sale August.

With new titles to choose from every month,
discover a world of romance in our books written
by internationally bestselling authors.

HARLEQUIN® *Presents*

It's the ultimate in quality romance!

Available wherever Harlequin books are sold.

www.eHarlequin.com

HPGEN06

SILHOUETTE *Romance*®

COMING NEXT MONTH

#1830 THE RANCHER TAKES A FAMILY—Judy Christenberry
Widowed rancher John Richey had sworn off women, but he would
do anything for his baby daughter—even remarry to give her a
mother. Debra Williams seemed the ideal choice for a marriage in
name only. Until she and her toddler son moved in and made his
house feel like a home again....

#1831 WINNING BACK HIS BRIDE—Teresa Southwick
Wealthy businessman Michael Sullivan needs advice on the most
important project of his career, and only one woman can help him—
Geneva Porter. But what man would want to work with the woman
who had left him standing at the altar? And could Michael still have
a vacancy for her...as his bride?

#1832 THE CINDERELLA FACTOR—Sophie Weston
The French château is the perfect hiding place for Jo—until its
owner, sardonic reporter Patrick Burns, comes home.... Patrick
thinks the secret runaway is a thief until he sees that Jo is hiding a
painful past. But as his feelings for her grow, can he prove to be her
Prince Charming?

#1833 THE BOSS'S CONVENIENT BRIDE—Jennie Adams
Claire Dalgliesh is stunned when her boss declares that he needs
a wife—and he's selected her for the job! Claire may have a huge
crush on Nicholas Monroe, but she's not going to walk up the aisle
with him—not without love. At least, that's what she thinks....